a
truth
worth tellin'

www.atruthworthtellin.com
Cover design by fresh frut, Hattiesburg, MS
Ramsay Publishing
PO Box 751
Missouri City TX 77459

ISBN: 0-615-30822-8
ISBN13: 9780615308227

Visit www.amazon.com to order additional copies.

a
truth
worth tellin'

toni teepell

To Daddy.

~(A TRUTH WORTH TELLIN')~

HOPE GOD KNOWS I didn't set out to be a liar. The first lie, the one Daddy knows about, was simple. It happened the day we moved from Minden to Pearl, Louisiana, when our landlady, Miss Clark, asked if it would just be Daddy and me living in her rent house. Before Daddy could take a breath, I answered yes, but Mama would be home soon. I then explained how Mama was taking care of her sick aunt, my Great-Aunt Margaret, out west. Daddy looked at me with his mouth open, but didn't say anything. That was the day I became a liar.

The problem with lying is my stomach. It's hurt ever since the day I met Miss Clark. At night I lay in bed worrying I'll forget my great-aunt's name, or the town she lives in, or a detail I've told about her house. The sad truth is I spend more time worried my deception will be found out, than concerned about Mama. Not sure what that makes me, but I'm certain it's worse than a liar.

"Maggie, let's go," Daddy says as he hangs up the phone.

He's through the kitchen and out the front door before I have time to get off the couch. With shoes in hand, I run to the truck praying it will crank. The '50 Chevy was bought the same day I was born, so in people years it's twelve, but in truck years it's around a hundred and ten. The thing should be in a field for dying vehicles, but then, Daddy would have to walk to work. I climb in and slam the door. "Daddy, did someone find Mama? Where is she?"

"Seven miles from the hospital."

He starts the engine and jiggles the switch to the heater that we surely don't need in May. He hits the dash. The heater didn't turn off the last time we were in the truck, but he hadn't hit the dash. Hot air continues to blow from the vents. It is a mystery why. We roll down the windows.

The weatherman predicted a moderate high in Pearl today. Said it would reach eighty-five degrees. He should take a ride in our truck. I'm sure it is over one hundred degrees and it's not yet noon. Should have brought a jug of water.

We drive the back roads in silence. To most folks these roads lead to a big city named Carlson, but for Daddy and me they lead to the state mental hospital. The hot air makes me sticky. Maybe if he hits the dash a little harder.

When we don't get trapped behind a tractor, the trip to Wakefield Hospital takes forty-eight minutes. For some reason, farmers around Pearl think they have the right to drive in the middle of the road. Dressed in costumes of overalls and straw hats, they smile and wave like it's Mardi Gras. Today there are no tractors in sight and Daddy has forgotten there's a speed limit.

I slide closer, slip my hand in his and rub the rough skin on his fingers. I love his hands. They're big and strong and make me think of Mama's stories about his military days. He was a boxer and traveled around to fight other military men. Seems a strange thing to do, but that's what the Navy wanted, so that's what he did. It was a whole year before anyone beat him. Mama said he quit after he got knocked out. Said he had a smart head and wanted to keep it that way.

"Who found her?" My voice sounds cranky like a gearshift.

"A Miss Delores," he says. "She lives off River Road."

"How did Mama get out? Don't they keep the doors locked at Wakefield?"

He glances my way. "Yeah, they keep 'em locked."

"Where did the lady find her, anyway?" I ask.

"In their shed," he answers.

The unfamiliar slump of his shoulders and grip on the steering wheel makes me think I should keep other questions to myself. I watch his face as he pulls onto Highway 67. The glare from the sun makes him squint so his eyes are nearly gone. They are dark brown, speckled with gold, and always show what he feels. Today he is tired.

I look away and stare out the window at pine trees, an occasional house, a tire swing and more pine trees. I close my eyes and wish to be on a beach feeling hot sand between my toes. The houses are smaller now. Some are boarded up and empty; others should have been abandoned long ago. Rocking chairs on front porches and chickens in yards tell of life. Daddy slows and turns onto River Road. An old colored man walks along the top of the levee carrying a fishing pole in one hand and a bucket in the other.

We travel down a long dirt road and I see a small shack in a grove of pecan trees. "Are you sure we're at the right place?"

"Think so." Daddy turns off the engine. "Do you want to stay in the truck?"

"I'll go with you."

When we reach the house, two girls are playing in the mud. One dips a plastic bowl in the water, while the other shapes pies. They look at me and smile.

Daddy's voice pulls me back. "I'm Frank Wall and this is my daughter, Maggie." He runs a hand along the top of his head, pushing back loose strands of brown hair.

She opens the screen door and smiles. Her skin, the color of coffee milk Mama used to make, glistens from the heat. "Hello, Maggie, my name's Delores." She motions toward the puddle. "Would you like to play with my girls? Y'all look about the same age. Josephine is ten and Lucinda is eight."

"I'm eleven almost twelve." I stand straight so she will see I look older than her girls.

"Well, y'all are pretty close. Would you like to play awhile?"

I look back at Lucinda and Josephine, who have not looked up from their pies. "No ma'am," I lie, "we're just here to get Mama."

"Come in then. She's in the back. Sorry I didn't call sooner, but it took me awhile to get her name. Saw the wristband, but couldn't get close enough to read it. Thought I was gonna have to call the hospital. Didn't want to do that on 'count of her being so scared. Can't say I blame her, that place scares me too."

I follow Daddy through the small living room. I can see the ground under the house through cracks in the floor. The kitchen is next and smells of cut pine.

"She's in there." Miss Delores steps aside so Daddy and I can go in first.

A quilt of yellow and blue squares covers a bed in the corner of the room. Two mattresses, with matching pink-flowered quilts, lay on the floor under the window. Mama crouches down next to a dresser. Dried mud covers her clothes and clings to her dark hair.

"Elizabeth, we're here to get you," Daddy says from the door.

Mama stands, backs against the wall and tries to disappear. "I'll die," she whimpers.

"I'm here to take you home." Daddy's voice is calm and soft.

He moves towards her.

"No, please," she sobs, "please let me stay with the angel. She'll take care of me."

For a moment I allow myself to believe her. Maybe she isn't crazy after all. Maybe she can see things and experience things others can't. Maybe this woman, with her brown skin and beautiful face, really is an angel sent from God. I look up into the woman's face and pray for a sign to confirm Mama's words. Miss Delores leans against the wall and looks down at the floor.

"There are no angels here," she says.

I look away.

Mama sees me for the first time. She stretches her arms toward me. I walk over, and she pulls me close. I wrap my arms around her and pretend she's like other mothers. Her body shakes as she cries softly. She smells musky from days with no bath. I close my eyes and imagine she's just come in from working in the yard. "We're here to take you home," I say.

"I knew you would come," she answers, rocking back and forth.

"Mama, don't squeeze, you're hurting me," I whisper.

"The angel is here to get my baby! Today my baby will go to heaven with the angels!" She laughs and squeezes harder.

It's hard to breathe. I struggle against her, but, before I cry for help, Daddy's strong arms break Mama's hold on me. He cradles her close to his chest. She doesn't fight as he lifts her into his arms and walks out the room.

I turn to leave, but stop and look at Miss Delores. "Thank you, ma'am," I mumble.

"Maggie, good luck with your mama," she says.

I nod and walk to the door. The girls are still in the mud, but I don't look at them. Instead, I walk straight to the truck and climb in the cab. Mama leans against Daddy. Tangled, dark, hair hides all but her mouth.

"It's all right, Elizabeth. We're going home." Daddy pulls

her closer.

He drives with one hand so he will not have to let her go. Half-way home, Mama's breathing slows and I know she's asleep. I lean my head against the worn seat and close my eyes, thinking of Miss Delores and her girls. I wonder what it's like to live in a house where you can see the ground through the floor; how it is to have a sister sleep next to you on a mattress, and what it's like to have a mama with skin the color of coffee milk.

When Daddy walks into my room, I'm across the bed thinking about what I'll say now that she's home. For the past two months, I've lied about Mama to anyone who will listen. The first day at Grant Elementary, Mrs. Vaughn made me stand in front of the sixth grade class and introduce myself. She said to tell about my family since we had just moved to town. For fifteen minutes I mostly talked about Mama and Aunt Margaret.

"They're in Santa Barbara, California," I said. "Aunt Margaret has a house right on the beach, so, when she's sleeping, Mama walks along the seashore. The ocean's cold so she doesn't swim, but sometimes puts her feet in the water. Mama can't call much, but writes letters almost every day. She can't wait to see our new home in Pearl."

I could have been talking about a foreign country the way they stared. At first I thought they didn't believe me, but then realized they were just impressed. I was the first person they knew with kinfolks living more than twenty-five miles from Pearl. I would have been impressed too, if it wasn't a lie.

"What ya doing?" Daddy sits on the edge of my bed.

"Nothing," I answer.

"She should sleep through the night."

"Good." I sit up.

"Maggie, I've got to work half a day tomorrow to make up some of the time I've missed. Then, I need to sign some papers at Wakefield."

I nod.

"You'll be all right?"

"Yeah, we'll be fine."

"If you need anything, go over to the Clarks'."

"Sir?" I look at Daddy and wonder if he has lost his mind too. What would he have me do at the Clarks'? Surely he doesn't expect me to tell them about Mama.

"I just can't bring her back to the hospital; not yet, anyway. Maybe she'll pull out of it on her own this time." The lines around his eyes go deeper than three days ago.

"Daddy, we'll be fine. I'll go to the Clarks' if I need anything."

"I love you, Mags." He kisses the top of my head.

"Love you too," I say.

"Lights on or off?" he asks.

"Off."

When the room is dark, I slip off my bed, kneel on the floor and recite a familiar prayer. "Lord, help Mama get well." I climb onto the bed and crawl under the covers. "If you get her well quick, I'll do my best not to lie anymore. Oh, and please forgive me for the lies I've already told. Amen." ⟿

⤙ TWO ⤚

THE FIRST TIME in our drive, it was the yard, not the house that caused me to hope. An old expectation that this move would be good for us all crept in as I scanned the elm, pine, dogwood trees and pink azalea bushes surrounding the small wood framed house. An enormous oak tree shaded the front rooms, an old barn in the back promised hours of adventure, and the most perfect tree house waited for me in the front yard. Next to the porch swing, the tree house has become my favorite place. It isn't fancy, like the one in Swiss Family Robinson, but there's space enough for two and a roof keeps out the rain.

I climb the ladder with book in hand and pray for an hour or two of uninterrupted reading. Daddy says I was born a reader. Don't think that's possible, but I can't remember a time without books. Last summer I read the entire Nancy Drew series. When I wasn't reading, I was creeping around solving made up crimes. The summer before that I read *Island of the*

Blue Dolphins and begged Daddy to move us to an island. This summer it's California. I've checked out all the books the library has on the subject, which is a total of three. Pearl's library is a couple of bookcases on Miss Annabelle Whitney's front porch. Sad, really, but, reckon it could be worse.

I lean back, eager to begin *Life in California*, but before the book is even open, a sound draws my attention to the gravel driveway. I watch, hidden by branches and leaves, as Sam leans her bike against an elm tree. She takes the bottom of her shirt and wipes off the blue seat. Her eyes never leave the bike as she walks to the front and wipes down the fender; now the back fender. She touches the seat once more and is done. Every time she parks the bike, it's the same routine.

Samantha Williams came with our house. The day we moved in, she was in the tree house. We waved, but she left before we could introduce ourselves. For the next week, every day after school, she was back. She didn't come in the yard, just rode her bike back and forth in front of the house. Once, I tried to speak, but she rode off without a word. Thought she might be deaf and dumb, like Helen Keller, but then after the third try, she talked back. It was another week before she got off her bike and two more before she came in the house. Now she comes and goes like she belongs.

"Sam, up here!"

A gust of wind blows through the trees and, for a moment, curls dance in circles above her head. Hands go up in protest, but the dance continues until the breeze dies down. She sighs and pushes the tangle of hair from her eyes.

Sam's hair is the biggest thing about her. Curls the color of copper pennies start at the roots and go all the way down the middle of her back. Looks like a comb will break right off if she tries to brush 'em. Maybe that's why she doesn't try. Probably broke a few good combs and gave up. The look on her face says she wants a rubber band or maybe a pair of scissors.

"Come on up," I say.

She makes her way up the ladder and crawls inside. Small streams of sweat curl down her face. She wipes them away with the sleeve of her shirt. "What ya doing?"

I shrug. "Why are you wearing a flannel shirt? It's only a hundred degrees out here."

"I dunno," she says. "Hey, is your daddy at work?"

I nod.

She stands, looks out the window, then sits back down. "I've got something."

Must be top secret. I scoot closer. "What?"

She reaches in the pocket of her jeans and pulls out a wad of tissue. She lays the bundle on the floor and unwraps one layer at a time. Her slow, careful movements make me think there's some poor creature under all the paper. Finally, with only one layer left a dark brown treasure begins to peek through.

My mouth flies open when it's unveiled. "Sam, where did you get that?"

"Wanted to sneak a cigarette from mama, but she counts 'em; got this from George."

"Who's George?"

Sam rubs the fat cigar with her fingers and says, "Mama's friend."

I know by the way she says *friend*, George isn't hers. "Won't he miss it?"

"He wouldn't miss his teeth if I took 'em out the jar."

"He keeps his teeth in a jar?"

Sam shrugs. "He's old."

"So what are you doing with it anyway?"

"Thought we could smoke it," Sam announces, as if suggesting we go to Sunday School.

Before I can answer, the cigar is in her mouth. She digs a box of matches from her pocket. "Come on Maggie, it'll be fun." A spark flies from the match before catching fire.

"Sam, you can't smoke!"

She grins and holds the fire to the cigar until the end glows a deep red. A trail of smoke curls toward the ceiling and a sweet smell fills the tree house.

"How do I look?" she asks between puffs.

The cigar looks the size of a small log in her hand. "You look silly."

She coughs. "Silly? I do not."

"Maybe a cigarette would work better," I say.

She rubs her eyes and coughs again. "You try."

Back in Minden, Pastor Jim preached about liars, thieves and other such bad people never seeing the Kingdom of God. At the end of each sermon, he threw in a few lines about drinkers and smokers. Wasn't clear if they would see the Kingdom of God or not, but he was clear that upstanding folks do not have vices. Eleven years and ten months old is probably not the best time to begin a vice.

I shake my head. "Better not."

Sam holds the cigar towards me. "Come on Maggie, just try."

I shake my head no.

"Just try it. Really, Maggie, one cigar won't kill you." She smiles.

Well, this is true, and besides, one puff won't make it a vice. My heart pounds like a drum at the Macy's Day Parade as I take the thing from her. I bring the cigar to my mouth and puff on it. Smoke flows from the end.

"Are you blowing on it? You have to breathe in, not out."

"Oh," I say. This is harder than it looks. I close my eyes and take in a deep breath. Smoke enters my mouth and bursts into flames as it reaches my throat and chest. Tears escape my eyes and slide down my cheeks. My insides will never be the same.

"That's better," Sam says.

I cough and take another deep breath. This one doesn't burn quite so much. By the fourth puff I'm no longer coughing and the flow of tears have stopped. My hands are bigger than Sam's so I can't look ridiculous like she does. I must look at least fourteen. I like cigars.

Sam stands and looks out the window. "You want to go to Murray's and look at magazines?"

"I better not."

"We'll be back before your daddy gets home from work."

I blow smoke out of my mouth. Small circles drift towards the window. I'm good at this. "Got chores to do," I say.

"Yeah, reckon I need to do my chores too. Guess I'll head home."

"Don't forget this." I move next to Sam and grab her arm.

She pulls away. "Ouch, Maggie, that hurt."

"Sorry, I didn't grab you that hard."

"It's all right." She brushes the lit cigar against the floor of the tree house and sticks it into her pocket. "I'll sneak this back in the cigar box."

"You don't want to smoke anymore?" I ask.

She smiles. "I hate smoking. Just wanted to see you with a cigar in your mouth, coughing your fool head off."

"I didn't cough that much. Think I may become a smoker."

She jumps from the ladder and climbs on the bike. "Yeah, Maggie, I'm sure you'll be stealin' cigars from Murray's next week."

"Sam, we'll go to town soon, promise."

I watch until she makes the curve on Clark Road, then sit and flip open my book to the San Francisco chapter.

"I'll live here one day," I say aloud so God can hear. "The Golden Gate Bridge will be right out my bedroom window. Daddy will have a good job, Mama won't need to live near the crazy hospital, and I won't ever have to lie again. Some day, everything will be perfect. ∼

~(THREE)~

DADDY HOPES FOR a miracle, but for the third straight day, Mama hasn't even gotten out of bed. The room is dark and smells like an old folks' home, so I pull back the green drapes and open the window. She's curled up in a little ball on top of the state quilt. The magnolia on the Louisiana square peeks out at the curve of her neck.

"Mama, what ya want for lunch?" She doesn't move. I look hard to see if she's breathing. "Mama, you need to wake up and eat."

She uncurls and sits up, but doesn't answer. She is a porcelain doll with pale skin and dark blue eyes the color of the sea. Thick, black hair hangs to the middle of her back, and even now, she's beautiful. Mama's beauty catches people by surprise, and makes them stare. That's how she's able to walk out of hospitals. They think she's visiting some poor soul, maybe someone she doesn't even know, because she looks kind and much too beautiful to be a patient in a state mental hospital.

"Mama, how about a sandwich? You didn't eat any of your eggs this morning." I wait for an answer, but she only stares. "I'm gonna fix us some lunch, okay?"

I force myself to walk in the kitchen. This is the second week of summer vacation, and I want to swim in a lake or sit under an oak tree and read a book. I open the refrigerator hoping to find banana splits and chocolate cake, but there's still only milk, eggs, butter, grape jelly, mayonnaise, and a pack of ham. Sure wish God would put a few angels in charge of stocking refrigerators. I take four slices of bread from the Sunbeam bag and lay them on the counter. The knife clangs against the jar as I scrape out the last of the Blue Plate mayonnaise.

Placing a sandwich on one of her good plates, the blue and white ones, the ones she saves for company, I walk back into the bedroom. She hasn't moved. I sit next to her, the plate in my lap.

"Mama," I say, "you need to eat. I made you a ham sandwich. Don't you want some?"

I break off a piece of bread and hold it close to her mouth. She looks into my eyes and I'm sure she sees me. I lean closer. "Eat this and I'll get you a glass of sweet tea."

"I don't want it," she whispers.

"Mama, please, you need -"

"I don't want that," she screams. "I know what you're trying to do!"

Before I can move, she has the plate in her hand and slings it across the room. The china shatters as it hits the wall.

"Get out of here and leave me alone! I don't want you in here!" She lies down and goes back into the ball.

My hands tremble as I pick up pieces of broken china and walk to the kitchen. I find the glue in the junk drawer with Daddy's hammer and screwdriver. Careful to squeeze just the right amount, I stick the pieces together, place the plate in the bottom drawer of my nightstand, and hope for the best.

❧

With a Coke in one hand, and a moon pie in the other, I make my fifth round. I walk from the kitchen to my bedroom, to the living room, and back to the kitchen. The whole trip takes less than a minute. The place is small, but at least clean. I sit on the kitchen counter and dangle my bare feet. A fresh coat of white paint covers the walls and lemonade yellow cabinets blend with the faded green Formica counter tops.

I watch from the counter as Daddy walks through the living room door. He stoops and unties his boots. Small bits of wood fall on the floor as he pulls off each one and sets them by the front door. Sweat and the brown leather have dyed his white socks beige. He sees me and smiles.

"How's your day?"

I smile, but don't answer.

"Is your Mama in bed?" He walks over and brushes bangs from my eyes, a habit he has gotten in since I began growing them out.

"I fixed a ham sandwich, but she wouldn't eat."

Daddy opens the Sunbeam bag and takes the last two slices. "Maybe I'll have better luck."

"We're out of mayonnaise and cheese. I made a list of groceries we need."

He grabs the peanut butter from the cabinet and opens the refrigerator. "Let me get your Mama something to eat, and then I'll go to Food Mart."

"Sunshine Food Mart," I correct. He grins at our joke. The only grocery store in town is a small cinder block building painted bright yellow inside and out. We've decided sunglasses should be handed out at the door.

I follow him to the back of the house and stand in the hall outside their bedroom. He talks to Mama in his calm voice and I hear her cry. He asks her to take a bite. She does not yell, so he asks again. A moment goes by with nothing, then he says, "Good Elizabeth, just eat a little more." ~

~(FOUR)~

RIGHT WHEN I'M about to call for a nationwide search, Sam shows up at my door. "Where have you been?" I walk on to the porch.

"Mama wouldn't let me come over."

"Five days is a record. Were you punished or something?"

"No." She wipes her face with the sleeve of her shirt.

My stomach begins its familiar ache. Mama's in bed, but may get up any minute. I walk to the side of the porch and sit on the swing. Sam stays by the closed door.

"You want to go in and play cards?" she asks.

"No," I say too quickly. "I thought we could go to Murray's."

"I don't want to ride back to town, it's hot."

"You wouldn't be so hot in a summer blouse. You can wear one of mine."

"I'm fine."

"Well, come over here and at least let me roll your sleeves up. Really, Sam, you need to stop dressing like it's winter."

"Said I'm fine," she mumbles.

"Suit yourself." I stare at my feet and say, "Thought it would be fun to look at magazines. The other day you wanted to go."

"All right, but at least give me a glass of water before I fall out right here." Sam reaches to open the door.

I'm across the porch before she can turn the knob. "I'll get you some. Why don't you wait on the swing?"

"I can get it."

"No, Daddy doesn't want friends over when he's not home." My face is on fire.

"Since when?" she asks.

"Since the other day. Just wait on the porch. I'll be right back." I walk in and close the door, leaving Sam to have a heat stroke all by herself. The house is quiet. I fill a glass with water and walk back outside.

Sam hasn't moved. She grabs the glass and gulps down the water.

"Want more?"

"No thanks." She leans against the door. "Why doesn't your daddy want me in your house? Did I do something to make him mad?"

One of the problems with lying is you can never tell just one. It usually takes at least three, but sometimes more. In order to be good, a notebook should be kept nearby at all times. There's nothing worse than forgetting your lies in the middle of a story.

"It doesn't have anything to do with you. He's been in a bad mood is all, maybe it's the heat."

Sam tilts her head and gives me a look that says she doesn't believe a word I just said. "Yeah, maybe," she mumbles.

"It's probably because he's missing Mama. She should be home soon. Aunt Margaret is doing much better. Yeah, he'll be back to normal when Mama gets back." I place the empty glass on the porch. "You ready to go?"

"Guess so," she mumbles.

Friends aren't supposed to lie to one another. I know this, but lie anyway, which makes me the worst sort of liar. We pedal in silence to Thompson Creek. Sam stops her bike on the bridge. She grabs a handful of rocks from the road and begins to throw one at a time into the muddy water below. I pick up two and toss them over.

"Guess what," she says between throws.

"What?"

"Johnnie Sue got herself suspended from the cheerleader squad."

"You mean, 'my daddy's on the school board' Johnny Sue?"

"That's the one. Last week at practice she got mad about something and told off Coach Westbrook."

"How long will she be punished?"

"She has to miss the first pep rally and game in the fall."

"That's it?" I ask. "Anyone else would have been kicked off the squad, but then no other cheerleader has a daddy on the school board. What I don't understand is why the kids in class bow down to Miss High and Mighty?"

"I have a theory about that." Sam grins. "It's her breasts."

"Sam!"

"She's the only girl in class with big breasts. You can't tell me you haven't noticed. I mean, there are some senior girls that would kill to have boobs her size. Yep, that's why the boys love her and the girls bow down in awe."

I giggle. "They are huge."

"That's not all." Sam pedals off the bridge. "Her grandfather has been the mayor of Pearl for the last hundred years. I mean, as if boobs and her daddy isn't power enough."

I pedal fast to catch up. "Put all that together, I guess she's the queen of Pearl."

Sam laughs. "Yeah, the wicked queen."

The water tower, with its bright orange letters, welcomes us to town. Murray's, located on Main Street, is in a remodeled building that used to sell livestock feed but now sells everything from paint to lipstick. Even has a pharmacy and soda fountain in the back. Don't know who decided to sell ice cream sundaes with tools and medicine, but in Pearl it seems to work.

We park our bikes on the sidewalk in front of the store and walk past a table piled high with kids' summer clothes. A poster board with yellow letters lets everyone know the clothes are half-priced. "Best Sale Ever" printed at the bottom corner of the sign. Flip-flops, plastic buckets, towels, and hats all thrown together in one big heap.

The door scrapes across the wood floor as I push it open and we're greeted with a blend of unpleasant orders. No matter how many times I walk in Murray's the smell of rubbing alcohol and a faded scent of grain takes me by surprise. I take shallow breaths through my mouth and follow Sam to the magazine rack on aisle three.

Sam grabs a *Better Homes and Gardens*. "Now, you have to look at every page before getting another one. My record is three."

"What are you talking about? What record?"

"It's a game I play with Miss Field. See how many I can look through before she comes along and says, 'Young lady, those magazines are for sale. If you want a free one, go to the library.' She says the same thing every time. Too dumb to think of anything new."

"That's a mean thing to say." I pick up a magazine. Sam is half-way through hers.

"It's the truth. I don't know how she ever got the job here. I can count back change better than her and I barely passed sixth grade math." She places the *Better Homes and Gardens* down and picks up *Life*.

"Did you look at every page?" I ask, still on page three of mine.

"You gotta look at the pages, not read 'em." The sound of approaching footsteps keeps me from complaining about the rules. "She's getting faster," Sam moans.

"Young ladies!"

I turn to meet the glare of a woman, who, in heels, is barely taller than Sam. Even the gray hair piled on top of her head doesn't make her tall enough to be an adult. A face, small and wrinkled, is home to dark eyes that seem to bore a hole right through me.

"Those magazines are for sale. If you want a free one, go to the library," she barks.

"I'm trying to decide which one I want," Sam says with a smile.

"Do you have any money?"

"No ma'am, we don't," I answer.

"That's what I thought. You two had better get out of here before I call the law."

"Now, Miss Field, you know you don't want to do that. We're not bothering anybody." Sam places the magazine back on the rack.

"You're bothering me!" She turns and stomps to the front of the store.

"She sure doesn't like you," I say.

"Why do you say that?"

"Let's see, the part about calling the sheriff kind of made me think y'all aren't friends."

"She treats all of her friends that way. Hey, go ask her when the new magazines will be in."

"Why? You go ask."

"Come on, Maggie. She won't tell me, remember she hates me." Sam rolls her eyes.

"Oh, all right." I walk slowly to the front of the store. Miss Field is perched on top of a stool, hands on the register, ready to ring up the next big sale. I creep closer and smile. "Excuse me, when will the new magazines be delivered?"

"You're new to Pearl, aren't you?"

I nod.

She looks down from her throne and motions for me to come closer. I lean against the counter, half expecting a bang on the head from her miniature sized hands. "You need to be more careful about the friends you choose."

"Ma'am?"

"You're not from around here, but you seem like a nice young lady. I'm just sayin' you better be careful who you spend time with. I'd hate to see you in trouble just because you don't know better."

I glance around the store to see Samantha walk out the door. "Yes ma'am thanks for the advice."

"And the next time you come in here, bring money to buy something."

I find Sam sitting on the curb in front of the barbershop.

"What'd she say?"

I sit beside her and mumble, "nothing much."

Sam grins and slides a chocolate bar from under her shirt. "Want some?"

"Where did that come from? Sam, did you steal that from Murray's?"

She shrugs. "It's not stealing if you're starving."

"It is so. Besides, you're not dying from hunger."

She rips open the wrapping. "How do you know? Anyway, they'll never miss one little candy bar. You want some or not?"

My mouth waters as I stare at the chocolate melting in Sam's hand. Can a person go to jail for eating stolen candy? Not sure of the laws in Pearl, and not wanting "thief" added to the title of "cigar smoking liar," I shake my head.

"Are you sure? It's really good."

"Sam, you shouldn't steal stuff. It's wrong."

"So it's wrong, big deal." She plops the last piece on my lap and licks her hand. "It's not wrong for you to have a bite."

I take a deep breath, look around for a sheriff, then stuff the chocolate into my mouth. "Promise you won't steal anything else."

"Yeah, sure, I promise." She climbs on her bike and pedals down Maine Street. "Hey, Maggie," she yells, "don't listen to ole Miss Field. She just doesn't like me, is all."

"Can't understand that, I mean, what's not to like?" I call out.

The whole way home I think of ways to get Sam to church. Hours of gospel songs and preaching might be just what she needs, but the thought of Samantha in the middle of a church makes me laugh out loud. ~

⤙ FIVE ⤚

THE NEXT MORNING Mama's voice draws me to the kitchen. "Maggie, come here, I need your help."

I find her by the stove. "What are you cooking?"

She stares into a large black pot. Steam rises toward the ceiling as water bubbles and boils. She throws forks, spoons, and knives into the pot and mumbles, "Tuberculosis."

"Mama, what are you doing?"

"We have to boil everything! Tuberculosis will kill me if I don't kill the germs."

"Mama, why don't we wait for Daddy? He'll know a better way to kill the tuberculosis."

"There's no other way. Everything must be boiled!" Her voice grows louder with each word. "I need you to help, not argue. Go get the sheets, no, no, go to the drugstore. Yes, that's it. Ride your bike to town and get some medicine. Tell him I have tuberculosis and need medicine. Ride your bike as fast as you can. Hurry, before I die."

"Mama, you'll be all right. The tuberculosis won't kill you," I say.

"You want me to die! You want me dead!" She crumbles onto the floor and sobs.

"Please get up. Everything will be all right." She doesn't move. "Please, Mama, get up and I'll go to the store. You have to get up, though. I'm not leaving you here on the kitchen floor."

I take her hands and pull until she stands. "Good, now go lay down on the couch until I get back." The tears have stopped, but she doesn't budge. "Mama, please go rest while I'm gone."

"Maggie," she whispers, "hurry before I die."

I brush the tears from my face, run out the door and jump on my bike. My stomach aches as I pedal down our gravel drive. I reach the pavement and speed up. What if she dies before I get back? Can a person die from an imagined disease?

The pothole appears from nowhere. I swerve, but not fast enough. The back tire leaves the pavement as the front tire disappears into the gap. I land hard in the middle of Clark Road. Blood trickles from my right knee.

"Lord, I need some help here." I'm face down on the black top and not sure what to ask for first. Heal the roads of potholes? Heal my knee? I take a deep breath and stand. "Just keep her alive, and help the man at the drug store be understanding."

I climb back on the bike, start out slower this time, and keep a look out for holes. It's one mile to the end of Clark Road, then exactly two miles to Thompson Creek. I pedal faster. Sweat drips from my face and the hot air burns my chest as I suck it down in fast gulps. I pass Moore Park and pick up the pace to the bridge. Unlike yesterday, I don't stop on the bridge and throw rocks into the creek. Today, I ride across without even a glance into the muddy stream below.

Twenty minutes later, I walk into Murray's. The store seems empty of customers and Miss Field is nowhere to be found. Maybe the whole town of Pearl won't find out why I'm here.

I take a deep breath and run through the gardening section, past shelves of fertilizer, to the pharmacy counter in the back left corner of the store. I ring the bell and practice the speech in my head until a man walks out of the office behind the counter. Staring up at him, I loose not only my speech but all the words I've spoken since a baby. He is tall as daddy — at least six feet — with skin the color of someone who spends every spare moment on a beach. Blonde hair frames a face that should be on the big screen, not in Pearl filling prescriptions.

"May I help you?" His smile reveals perfect, white, teeth.

My face burns as I remember leaving the house without brushing my teeth, or hair for that matter. I stare at the shelf of cough syrup and try to remember my name.

"Miss, do you need something? What happened to your knee?"

I glance up to see that same smile and eyes the color of emeralds. Still, no words will form.

"Are you looking for antiseptic and band-aides? Would you like a pad and pen so you can write down what you need?"

Oh great, he thinks I can't talk. Now would be a good time to have super powers and disappear.

He opens drawers in search of a pen. "Let's see, here's one. Now, where's that pad?" He opens another drawer.

"I don't need to write anything," I say, barely above a whisper.

He places his square-rimmed glasses on the counter and rubs his eyes. "So, how can I help you?"

I survey the store for other customers, then look back at the cough syrup.

"My name is Ben, but everyone around here calls me Doc. What's your name?"

"Maggie Wall." My voice is back.

"Wall, oh you and your dad are renting the Clark's place. You moved in a couple of months ago, didn't you?"

"Yes, sir," I say.

"So how can I help you, Maggie Wall? Don't worry; this conversation is just between you and me."

"I need some medicine for my Mama." I smile.

"Do you have a prescription?"

"No sir, but I need some tuberculosis pills." I am no longer smiling and my tongue is sticking to the roof of my mouth.

"So you need some medicine for tuberculosis, but don't have a prescription?"

"Yes sir, my mama doesn't have tuberculosis." I take a deep breath. "She thinks she does. I could buy some cold medicine, but she'd know. She's still smart. I was hopin' you could give me something in a real medicine bottle. You know, make it say something like, to cure tuberculosis take these pills."

Doc stares and tilts his head from side to side. His smile is gone.

"Another thing, I don't have any money. My daddy will come up later and pay what we owe," I say quickly.

He clears his throat and disappears into the office. I stare at the row of blue and green bottles under the cough syrup until my eyes begin to cross. I turn to leave.

"Maggie, I think this will do the job." Doc walks from behind the counter and kneels down so his eyes are level with mine. "Your mama's name is not on the label, but it should work. It's vitamins."

The bottle has a label with typed directions to take one pill every day for the treatment of tuberculosis. I smile. "This will work just fine. How much do we owe?"

"No charge," Doc says.

"Thank you." My face is on fire again. This man really should be in the movies. I back away before he notices my teeth.

I pull into our driveway confident this medicine will cure any disease Mama thinks she has. I lean my bike against the wood house and walk inside waving the bag. "Mama, I'm back. Got your medicine," I call.

She comes out of the kitchen with rubber gloves. "Put these on," she says.

The yellow gloves fly across the room, bounce off my chest and fall to the floor. I pick them up and follow her to the kitchen. An empty bottle of Lysol and a half jug of milk are on the table.

"What about your medicine? Mama, you want your medicine?"

She points to a bucket by the sink. "They said this will get rid of the germs. We have to clean everything. Be careful, that's all we have."

I pull the gloves on and fish a rag out of the bucket. I'm not sure what the germ killing potion is, but it smells horrible. "Mama, I don't think we need to wipe this on anything."

She bangs the side of her head with her fist. "It's the only way," she yells.

"All right, I'll clean everything. Why don't you take your medicine and go lay down?"

She sits in the kitchen chair and runs her fingers over the paper sack. A little over an hour ago she was going to die without this medicine, now she won't even open the bag. I shake my head and rub the rag along the cabinet. The smell makes me want to gag.

I don't remember the first time Mama got sick, I was only two, but by the time I was four the doctors decided Mama was schizophrenic. For as long as I can remember, she has spent a few months each year in a mental hospital. Doctors give her different pills to take and always seem surprised when she gets better. Some years she's sick more months than she's well. It's been five months now, which is about the time living with the sickness gets hard.

We do all our living when we have the well Mama. Monopoly games or cards take over most evenings. Some nights we lie in the backyard and look up at the stars. Once we played hide and seek in the house. Ran like we were out in the fields, laughing until our bellies hurt, tears rolling down our faces. Her laugh is better than anything in the whole world.

I glance toward the kitchen table. She's still there making sure I don't miss any germs. I drag the bucket into the living room, dip my rag once more into the putrid smelling liquid, and wipe the couch. With my back facing her, I close my eyes and think of the last good day together, December twentieth, our Christmas tree day.

No matter where we live, every December twentieth, we go into the woods and cut down a pine tree. Daddy and I always choose a tall, full pine that we know will make a beautiful Christmas tree. Mama always picks a lopsided tree with a few missing branches. She somehow convinces us that her tree will look perfect in our living room and Daddy drags the thing home. Each year we decorate our underdeveloped pine, careful to face the barest part to the wall, and each year end up with a tree that barely keeps the blue and red ornaments off the floor.

Don't know why she feels the need to rescue scrawny trees. I guess some folks open their homes to unwanted cats and dogs; we are the home for unwanted Christmas trees. Last year was no exception.

※

We decided to look for it early that morning. Daddy and I waited in the yard, stomping our feet to keep warm.

"This year let's get a big tree," I said.

"I figure a six or seven footer will look just about right in the living room. Maybe even a . . .," he stopped mid-sentence when the

screen door opened. His eyes landed on Mama and didn't leave as she walked across the yard.

She was dressed in her favorite slacks, Daddy's flannel shirt, and rubber boots. All but a few dark curls were pulled back in a ribbon. "Frank, do you have my coat?"

Daddy held up her jacket and smiled. She kissed him and slipped into the wool jacket.

"Ready?" Daddy asked.

Mama nodded. "When we get back I'll make some hot chocolate. Maggie, would you like that?"

"Sounds good," I answered.

Mama threw her arm around Daddy's waist and they headed across the yard. I trailed behind listening to Daddy's soft words and Mama's giggles. We slipped through the barbed wire that once fenced in cattle, and by the time we entered the woods they were silent.

Sunlight poured through the pine, elm and birch trees casting a golden shadow on their trunks. The occasional crunch of dead leaves under our feet was the only sound as we walked through the forest in search of the perfect pine. I spotted Mama's tree before she did. It was small, four feet or so, and the only one around with a few missing branches.

"Maggie, here's a nice one," Daddy said. He stood next to a six-foot beauty. It was perfect.

I ran around the tree. "This one's great! Mama, don't you think?"

"Uh-huh," she said.

Daddy smiled and winked at me. We watched as she walked around the lopsided tree.

"Frank, what do you think of this one?"

"That little thing? Kind of scrawny," Daddy answered.

"Yeah, but it has promise. With a few decorations, it would work," Mama said.

"I don't know Elizabeth. Why don't we get a bigger tree this year?"

"Yeah, this year you and Maggie pick," she said still staring at her tree.

I walked over, slipped my hand in Daddy's and smiled. "Mama, that little tree would look good in our living room."

"You think so?" She smiled.

"Yes ma'am, it will be fine."

Daddy squeezed my hand. "All right then, guess that's our tree."

Mama walked over and cupped my face in her hand. "I love you Mags."

"Love you too," I said.

She gave me a quick kiss on the cheek. "We can string popcorn this year. Won't that look nice?"

"Yes ma'am, popcorn might help."

❧

Daddy's voice pulls me back from the forest. "Elizabeth, what's going on here?"

We are in the bathroom, me on the floor wiping the cabinet, Mama standing in the doorway. She walks out without a word. We hear the bedroom door slam shut. I take off the gloves and drop them in the bucket.

"She thinks she has tuberculosis. I've been cleaning everything with some magic potion. The furniture will never be the same."

"Maggie, I'm sorry."

"I'm tired; think I'll go rest a while." I leave him to deal with the bucket and walk to my bedroom. I close the door, climb onto my bed, and even though it is at least eighty degrees in my room, pull the covers up to my chin. If ever there was a day to go back to bed, this is it.

"Lord, why are we here in Pearl anyway? How did we end up in this life?" I look up at the ceiling and wait for an answer. "Any communication would be great. A dove, a burning dresser, even an angel sent to earth with a trumpet."

A knock at the door nearly sends me to the floor. Does God knock?

"Maggie?"

I roll over and put the pillow on my head. I feel him on the edge of the bed.

"Maggie, I'm so sorry. I would have never ..."

I interrupt, "It's all right, really, I'm fine."

"Yeah, then why do you have a pillow on your head?" Daddy asks.

I push the pillow aside and sit up. He brushes bangs from my eyes. I think of the Christmas tree day and the way Daddy looked at Mama.

"Do you think I'm pretty?" The question doesn't really count because fathers would cut out their tongues before admitting they have ugly daughters. I ask anyway.

"Yes, you have your mother's eyes."

He could lie better than this. "I have green eyes, not blue."

"Yeah, but your eyes are almond shaped just like your mama's. You have her nose, thin and straight, and her dimples when you smile."

"Except that I have dull brown hair and a face full of freckles. If I get one more they will blend together into one big dot," I moan.

"Freckles go away." He looks down at a book in his hands and says, "Got this for you."

I crawl out from under the covers. "What is it?"

"Milton, a man I work with, gave this to me. He knows you're interested in California. It's a travel guide."

I thumb through the paperback. "How does he know I like California?"

"Oh, I told him. We work together most days. He and his wife don't have any kids. They wanted 'em, just never happened. He likes hearing about you."

"Tell him thanks," I say.

Daddy picks at a thread on the quilt. Strands of brown hair fall in his eyes. I want to say something to ease the concern in his face, but nothing comes, so I flip the pages of my travel guide.

"Why do you like California so much?"

"Well, it has an ocean and mountains. Lots of people are there, so it must be a good place to live. Weather is nice too. In San Francisco you can watch sea lions right from a pier."

"You read that in one of your books?"

"Yeah, and there's this crooked street called Lombard Street. No other street in the world is as crooked."

"I've been there."

"When were you in San Francisco?" I am amazed. "Why don't I know this?"

"Guess I didn't think about it until just now. I was there about a month when I was in the Navy. It's a nice place, but too many people."

"Daddy, I can't believe you've been there. That's where I want to live, right by the Golden Gate Bridge. Did you see the bridge?"

"Yeah, I might even have a picture or two."

"Can I have 'em?"

"Sure, if I can find them."

"Maybe we can go there someday. You could show me around."

"Sure, Mags, we'll go one of these days." He stands and walks to the door. "I'm going to take your mama to the Mental Health Clinic in Carlson tomorrow morning."

"What about work?"

"I'll go in late. Maybe the doctors can change her medicine."

"Maybe," I mumble.

Daddy waits for me to ask if I can go, but I say nothing. "Maggie, will you be all right by yourself?"

I nod.

"You sure?" he asks.

The lie slips out before I can stop myself. "I've got a book to read for school." I look away from Daddy's stare. He knows.

"We should be home sometime after lunch."

I reckon Daddy needs a reason for me to stay home more than he needs to teach me the importance of honesty.

"Maggie, your Mama will be well soon."

"I know." I smile until he leaves my room. ❧

～ SIX ～

THE NEXT MORNING the sound of a gun pulls me from a dream of the ocean. I jump up, heart pounding, and stumble to the window. The boom is only the backfire of the exhaust as Daddy turns onto Clark Road. I climb back in bed thankful my heart didn't explode, and begin my daily search for spiders. A giant oak lives right outside my window which keeps the box fan off until noon. For this I'm thankful, because the shrill sound of the fan causes my head to ache, but the tree also provides a home to all types of living creatures. Some get the bright idea to come inside for a visit. I don't mind the one or two lizards that make their way in, lizards tend to stay to themselves, but spiders are a different story. If left alone, they would take over the entire world, spinning webs from one end to the other. That's why I stomp on every one I see; don't want to become a visitor in my own room.

I sit up to inspect things more closely. Butter-colored walls, bright yellow curtains and bedspread give the room a wide-awake look. When we moved in everything was an ugly faded blue, barely a color at all. I picked the new color down at Murray's and Daddy painted the whole room our first weekend in the house. Found the curtains and bedspread on sale in a second hand shop the next week. I scan the wall by the window; no spiders today. The smell of Mama's cleaning potion must have run them out of the house.

I make my way to the kitchen and grab a cup from the cabinet. A pot of coffee, still warm, sits on top of the stove. I fill my cup with the black liquid and sit at the table. Daddy doesn't let me drink coffee, but after my near-death experience I'm sure he would make an exception. I add two teaspoons of sugar and pour the cream until it's the shade of milk chocolate. After one sip I add a little more cream and two more teaspoons of sugar. Any more cream and it will officially be coffee milk, which is not the same as a real cup of coffee. I take another sip, pleased with the syrupy sweetness that fills my mouth. Wonder how a cigar would taste with my coffee?

"I am headed straight to hell," I say to the empty kitchen.

"Hey Maggie, you in there? Maggie, you home?"

I jump up and run to the back door. "You scared me to death! Second time this morning I've just about had a heart attack." I open the front door to see Sam standing on the porch steps. Her dress is dirty and hair is a mess, which isn't all that out of the ordinary, but her face looks like she's been in a boxing match. Her right eye is swollen almost shut and her lip is puffy. Dried blood is on the corner of her mouth. "What on earth happened to you?"

"Can I come in?" she asks.

"Sure." I push open the screen door.

"Thanks, Maggie." Her voice is soft.

"Come sit at the kitchen table. You want a Coke, or water, or something? Have you had breakfast?" I don't know exactly what to offer a beat up person.

She mumbles a reply that I can't understand so I fill a glass with water and set it on the table. She gulps it down.

"Want more?" I ask.

She shakes her head.

"Sam, do you need a doctor? You look pretty bad."

"I don't need no doctor. Can I stay awhile?"

"Sure."

We sit and stare at the floor. Finally she says, "She was drunk. That's why she did it. She wouldn't hit me if she wasn't drunk."

"Sam, who did this to you?"

"My mama," she mumbles.

"Your own mama did this to you?"

"Came in early this morning so drunk she could barely walk. I tried to help her to bed and she got mad. Wouldn't have done it if she wasn't so drunk."

I've never been around a drunk mama before, must be a little like a crazy mama. "Have you had a bath?"

She looks down at her dress. "Today? No, not since Monday, she's been gone all week."

"Well then, I'm going to fix you a hot bath. You'll feel better clean." Don't know if this is true, but it's the only thing I can think to say.

Sam follows me to the bathroom and watches as the tub fills with water. I place shampoo beside the tub with hope of clean hair, and hand her a dress from the clothes basket. She stands, staring at the water as I close the door. Whether she actually gets in is her decision. She might be one of those kids who don't like baths. Hopefully, though, she stays dirty because the drunk mama never taught her to stay clean.

Back in the kitchen I search for food. The milk bottle has barely a mouth full left, so cereal is out. I grab the Sunbeam bag, peanut butter and grape jelly. Thank the Lord for peanut butter and jelly sandwiches. We would all starve to death without them. I make three sandwiches: one for me, one for her, and an extra just in case she's as hungry as she looks.

"Maggie, thanks for letting me wear your dress."

She leans against the cabinet for support, pale but clean. Wet, red hair hangs down her back in one big ringlet. My dress hangs off her shoulders a little, but doesn't look half bad. Cleaned up, Sam looks good, almost pretty.

"You look nice." I motion for her to join me at the kitchen table. "You ought to bathe everyday, whether she's there or not. Here, I made you a sandwich. I know it's early for lunch, but we're out of milk."

Nodding, she takes a bite of her sandwich. She doesn't talk until it's gone. "Thanks," she says.

"Want another one? I made an extra." I hand her the sandwich and take a bite of mine. "Maybe you should stay here," I say between bites.

"No, I'll go home later."

"Daddy may want you to stay here. I mean, it ain't right what your mama did."

Sam jumps up. The extra sandwich and chair land on the floor. "No, you can't tell!" Her voice shakes and her eyes fill with tears. "The law will find out and they'll put me in a foster house."

"What's a foster house?"

"A place they put kids nobody wants. My mama was raised up in one. She talks about it when she drinks. A foster house is terrible."

Must be plum horrible if it's worse than living with the drunk mama. "I won't tell," I say.

"You swear? You swear you won't tell?" Her face has turned the bright red of the apples on the plastic tablecloth.

"Cross my heart, stick a needle in my eye." I make the sign of a cross on my chest. "Gee, Sam, you need to calm down. You're making me nervous."

She rights the chair and picks up the sandwich. "Sorry."

"Now look here, I won't tell Daddy, but you have to promise me something."

She sits down and rubs the eye that isn't swollen. "What?"

"That you'll come here if she ever does anything like this again."

"She won't do it again," Sam whispers.

"I'm gonna take mine back," I say.

Her eyes fill with tears again. "All right, anyway, you can't take a promise back."

This is true, but I'm not going to let on she's right. I get the deck of cards from the kitchen drawer. "You want to play Battle?"

"Guess so. Hey, who was that lady with your daddy? I saw 'em leave from the tree house."

I shuffle the cards. "That was Mama."

"She's home from California?"

I nod. "Let's play Fish instead."

"Where were they going?"

I look away and say, "Carlson to shop."

"On a work day?" she asks.

Sam should be a detective with all of her questions. "Yeah, Daddy wanted to spend some time with Mama. They'll make a day of it, you know, shop a little and have lunch."

"That's nice. I wish…," she stops and rubs her good eye again.

A burning sensation creeps across my face and that all too familiar ache in my stomach returns. Daddy says every person on earth is born with a device that lets them know right from wrong. Some call it their conscience, others say it's their inner voice; he calls his a gift from God. I don't know what to call mine, but I do know it lives in my belly.

Not so long ago I would argue that prisons, like Alcatraz, are filled with folks who either weren't born with the device or were born with defective ones. Just now though, with this lie to Samantha, I know that isn't true. I have the same thing Daddy has inside him, and it wasn't broken at birth either. No, I broke the thing two months ago.

Most of my big lies were told to strangers. They were wrong, just like the ones I'm filling the kitchen with now, but easier to tell. Sam is my best friend, my one and only friend in Pearl, so lying to her should be hard. The strange thing is my stomach hurt worse with my first lie. In fact, each lie hurts less. A few more months on this road and my stomach won't know the lies from the truth.

I take a deep breath and mumble, "They didn't go shopping."

"Where then?" she asks.

"You promise not to tell what I'm about to say? You swear on your mama's grave?"

"My mama's grave? She don't have no grave."

"It's just a saying. It means this is an important promise that can't be broke."

"Oh, well then, I swear on my mama's grave." Sam makes the sign of the cross like she saw me do.

"He took Mama to see a doctor. She wasn't in California. She's been in Wakefield."

Sam's mouth flies open. "The crazy hospital?"

I nod. "She has a sickness in her head."

Sam stares at me for a moment, mouth still open. "What does it do?"

"She hears voices and sees things. Sometimes it makes her yell and say things she doesn't mean. Sometimes she cries and won't get out of bed." I shuffle the cards again. "Sometimes it makes her want to be dead."

"Oh." She glances toward the floor.

"Daddy's taking her to the mental health clinic. They'll give her a different medicine." I deal each of us seven cards. "You'll like Mama when she's not sick. The well mama's a good mama."

"How long until she's well?"

"Soon," I say. "Now remember, Sam, you can't tell. People don't need to know about her sickness, they won't understand."

She nods and picks up her cards.

"Got a seven?" I ask.

Sam grins. "Go fish."

I doubt the truth will forever flow from my mouth, but at least I've been honest with Sam. I pray she can keep a secret.

❧

An afternoon rain comes just after Sam pedals onto Clark Road. She'll be soaked by the time she makes it home. I lie on the couch and close my eyes. My breath matches the slow, rhythm of the rain on the tin roof. I picture the ocean from my dream and imagine the waves hitting the shore. Sleep is about to come when the grandfather clock in the corner of the room bongs. The vibrations just about knock me to the floor. What is it today? I sit up and look toward the sound.

The clock, like the rest of our furniture, doesn't match our house. The poster beds, sofa, china and the rest are antiques from Mama's dead parents. Don't think Daddy cares for the old stuff, but he doesn't complain when we haul everything from house to house. The dining room furniture wouldn't even fit in the kitchen of our last house. It took up the kitchen and most of the living room. Mama finally decided to sell it, but cried when the lady drove off with her table and twelve chairs. That day won't soon be forgotten.

⚜

We saw the cloud of dust before the fancy car. Daddy and I watched from the front porch as a car and two trucks emerged from the cloud onto our drive.

Daddy whistled. "A '59 Caddy. That would be a whole year's salary. Sure is a beautiful automobile."

Before the sedan stopped rolling, the driver, a colored man in a suit and hat, jumped out and opened the back door. His hound dog face and the fact that he was too tall for his pants, took away from the fancy clothes.

"Who is this lady, anyway?" I whispered.

Daddy shrugged. "Afternoon," he said to the man.

The man nodded as he helped his passenger, a middle-aged woman, out of the car. She tugged on the bottom of her dress and straightened the belt around her waist as she walked over to Daddy.

"Good afternoon, are you Mr. Wall?"

"Yes ma'am," Daddy answered with a smile.

"I'm here to look at the furniture. Your wife said it's a 1920's piece from Italy." She patted the tightly wound bun at the back of her neck.

"Yes ma'am sure is."

"I know antiques," she said. "How did you end up with it?"

Before Daddy could answer, Mama walked out on the porch. "Mrs. Blake, have you met my husband, Frank, and our daughter Maggie? Would you like a glass of tea or maybe a cup of coffee?"

"No thank you," Mrs. Blake answered.

"Would the drivers care for anything?" Mama asked.

"No, they're fine. Can I see the table?"

"Sure, come in." Mama held the screen door open and winked at Daddy as Mrs. Blake walked inside.

Daddy mumbled something under his breath and grabbed my hand. We walked inside as Mama explained how she ended up with the furniture.

"My parents made several trips to Europe in the forties to furnish our home. This set came from a shop in Rome."

Mrs. Blake ran her gloved hand along the edge of the table. "It is exquisite. I live on a sugar plantation south of Ruston. This will look beautiful with the rest of my antiques. Anywhere would be better than this. I mean, it is just so out of place here."

Daddy put his arm around Mama's waist. "Elizabeth, we don't have to sell your table."

"Frank, Mrs. Blake is right, it does look out of place," Mama said.

"We won't always live in a small house. We can move to a house with a bigger kitchen," Daddy said.

"Really, Mr. Wall, this deserves to be in a formal dining room, not a kitchen." Mrs. Blake pulled a wallet from her purse.

"Mama, the table's fine here." I stared at Mrs. Blake and would have given everything we owned if Mama could trade places with this woman and her black Cadillac. Miss High and Mighty could spend most of a year in the state mental hospital while Mama dressed in fancy clothes and lived on a plantation. I smiled at the thought of Mrs. Blake in the crazy hospital. She wouldn't last a day.

Daddy let go of Mama and walked toward Mrs. Blake. "Ma'am, I'm going to have to ask you to put away your money."

"Mrs. Wall, I will pay double the asking price."

Mama grabbed Daddy's hand. "That is very kind. Your men can go ahead and load the furniture."

"Elizabeth, are you sure?" Daddy asked.

Mama nodded and took Mrs. Blake's money. We watched from the porch as the men went in and out of the house hauling the furniture to the truck. The entire time the two men never even glanced our way. Their eyes were either on the furniture or the floor.

"Let me get the men some water," Mama offered.

Mrs. Blake motioned the men into the trucks. "No, they're fine. We have to get back."

Anyone with sense could see the men weren't fine. Even Hound Dog was drenched, and he was just standing guard at the car.

I moved toward the door. "I'll get some."

Before I could get back with the water, the caravan was headed down our drive. We walked into the house and stared at the empty kitchen. It seemed strange to have so much space.

"I wouldn't work a day for that lady. I'd rather starve," I said.

"Now Maggie, mind your manners," Daddy said.

"Did you see the way she treated her workers? She acted like she was the Queen of England or something. Daddy, you wouldn't work for her either."

I glanced over at Mama and waited for her be-kind-to- others speech, but instead she buried her face in her hands and began to cry.

Daddy grabbed the truck keys from the counter. "Elizabeth, it's not too late. I can get the furniture back."

"No Frank, I'm being silly."

Daddy pulled Mama close. "You're not being silly. You ate every meal at that table growing up. It means something to you."

"But it's too big and we need the money."

Daddy cupped Mama's face in his hands. "Elizabeth, we've needed money before and done just fine. We'll manage without selling your table."

As much as I hated that table, I wanted it back. How many times had I watched Mama polish and shine the thing as she hummed Amazing Grace?

"I love you, Frank Wall," Mama said.

"I'll go after them. I can get the table back. "

"I'm fine with this. Really, I am." Mama kissed him and smiled. "I can live without a piece of furniture. All I need are the two of you."

"Elizabeth, we're not doing this again. You can't sell any more of your furniture." Daddy gently kissed her mouth.

"I promise, unless we need the money," she laughed. "Now, how about setting up our new table?"

Our new dinette set was an aluminum table and chairs with red padded seats found in the attic. Daddy cleaned it up and Mama placed an apple-covered tablecloth on top.

She stood back and looked it over. "That doesn't look bad."

"At least now we don't have to climb over the table to get the milk out of the refrigerator," I said.

"Ain't that the truth?" Mama shook her head and laughed. "Now, how about we try out our new table? How does cake and milk sound?" ~

～ SEVEN ～

I OPEN MY EYES to the sound of Daddy's voice. "Maggie, honey, wake up."

"Huh, what time is it?" I rub my eyes and sit up. I'm stiff from lying on the sofa too long.

"It's late, around 9:30. Have you been sleeping long?" Daddy sits next to me and strokes the back of my hair.

"Yeah, the rain must have put me to sleep. Where's Mama?"

"She's in bed."

He slumps against the back of the sofa. His clothes are wrinkled and there's a coffee stain on his pants. For the first time, I notice gray hair mixed in with his side burns. Thirty-four is too early for gray.

"What did they say?" I ask.

"They want to admit her to County General at the end of next week."

No wonder his hair has turned gray, County General costs money. "Why not the state hospital?"

"Doctor wants to try some other treatment, and they don't do it at Wakefield. He says this treatment will help her."

"What kind of treatment?"

"Called it shock treatments. They'll put electrical shocks through your Mama's brain. The doctor said this sort of thing has helped a bunch of folks."

"People with the same sickness as Mama?"

"Yep, that's what the doctor said. He'll do a total of eight treatments in two weeks, and then she'll go to Wakefield." He grabs my hand. "You want to sit on the porch for awhile?"

I follow Daddy outside. We watch the darkness and listen to crickets. The scent of rain still hangs in the air, which means there will be another shower. A sparrow makes its way to the bottom step, looks around, then flees when he catches a glimpse of the occupied swing.

"What did you do today?" Daddy asks.

"Sam came over and we played cards."

"You know I don't mind Samantha coming over, but I don't want you going to her house."

"Why?" Sam has never invited me, but if she does I want to go.

"She doesn't live in a safe area."

"What do you mean? It's safe enough for Sam. I should be able to go over to my friend's house." This is not important to me, but I argue anyway.

"Maggie," Daddy takes a deep breath, "it's not open for discussion."

"Well, it's not fair. I should be able to go to her house. Am I a prisoner now, not able to leave home?" I am close to tears.

"Did you eat anything for dinner?" he asks.

I shake my head. "Not hungry, and besides you didn't answer my question. Daddy, this is not fair!"

"Watch your tone, young lady." His voice is harsher than normal.

I'm up from the swing and in the house before he can say another word. Slamming the door to my room, I throw myself on the bed. What's wrong with me? I've never even thought about going to Sam's before now.

He opens the door without a knock and sits next to me. I am much too old to be held, but I lay my head on his shoulder anyway and close my eyes.

"It's not fair," I say.

"I know," he whispers.

After a long while, he asks, "Did I ever tell you about meeting your mama for the first time?"

I shake my head no, even though the day is etched in my mind as if I were beside him the moment he said hello.

"Her family had just moved to town. They stopped to get gas at the service station where I worked. That's when I saw her. She smiled while I pumped the gas, and I swear she was the prettiest girl I'd ever seen in my life. While her parents talked with Mr. Bridges, the owner, I hung by the car and washed the windows. She introduced herself and asked questions about the high school. I don't remember what I said, but she thought it was funny." He stops and clears his throat. "Two months later we were dating. She graduated valedictorian of her class that year and received a full scholarship to college. Her parents were horrified when she turned it down to marry me. Mr. and Mrs. Broussard had big plans for their only child and I don't think they ever forgave me for interrupting 'em. I wanted to put off the wedding so she could get a degree, but your mama wouldn't hear of it. Said she couldn't wait four years to get married and promised to attend college later."

"Why didn't she ever go?"

"You were born a year after we married, and two years after that, she got sick."

I nuzzle closer. "Daddy, I'm sorry about before."

"Me too," he says. "How about some supper? I'll make my world famous pancakes."

"Sure," I say, my head still on his shoulder.

"Oh yeah, I almost forgot. Found this for you." He pulls a small square photograph from his pocket.

"The Golden Gate Bridge!" I spring from the bed and grab the picture.

"Yeah, found it last night. It's kind of small, but you can make out the bridge."

"Do you know this is the longest suspension bridge in the world? There's enough cable to circle the equator three times."

"No kidding?" He smiles.

"Do you think we can go there, you know, on vacation?"

"Sure Mags, one day."

"Sam could come. She would love San Francisco. We'll go to the pier and Lombard Street and of course to the bridge. Maybe we can even try some lobster." I stare at the photograph. "Mama would like it too."

Thunder rumbles in the distance. This will be more than a shower. I wonder when we'll go on vacation. The bigger question is how. San Francisco might as well be across the globe in China or somewhere since Daddy's truck barely makes it out the driveway.

"Do you think these electrical treatments will do some good?"

"It's worth a try. Maybe this is just what your mama needs." He squeezes my hand. "How about those pancakes?"

Daddy's pancakes, small with crispy edges and golden brown in the middle, are the best.

"I'll get the butter and syrup." ❧

~ EIGHT ~

BY MORNING THE rain has stopped, the sky is clear and it's sticky hot. The pot of coffee on the stove is cold, so I drink a glass of milk and eat an apple. The rent envelope, with instructions to drop it by the Clarks', sits on the counter by an unopened box of Honey Flakes.

I slip on clothes and run the brush through my hair. I hope one morning to find long, curly hair on my head. So far, it still hangs to my shoulders without a single wave. With an extra heap of Colgate on my toothbrush, I brush extra hard and long. I smile into the bathroom mirror to find teeth still not as white as Doc's. How does anyone get his teeth so white? I push bangs out of my eyes. Daddy's right, they are shaped like Mama's. Don't agree with the nose though. My nose is much shorter and kind of turns up at the end. Maybe when I grow up it will turn into a thin, just right nose.

"I'm going, I'll find a way," Mama calls.

I find her in the kitchen by the stove. The first thing I notice is black hair that no longer falls to the middle of her back. Now, most hangs just below her shoulders. In back, the hard to reach pieces sneak past a bit longer. None of it is even. Her navy blue church dress clings to a slender body that *Life* magazine would love to photograph. The hair, however, would keep photographers away.

"Mama, why are you dressed for church?"

"The mission, got to get to town," she mumbles.

"We'll have to wait for Daddy," I say, hoping this will be enough to keep her home.

"No, no, have to get a telegram to President Kennedy. Walk, that's it, I'll walk."

I glance down at her heels and moan. "Mama, let's wait for Daddy. You don't want to mess up your church shoes."

"I have to go now!" She walks out the front door without a glance in my direction.

The thought of Mama in town announcing her mission to everyone she sees makes my stomach ache. Daddy will have to move us again. I will not step foot in Pearl after this disaster. I stuff the rent envelope in my pocket and run after her.

The Clarks' driveway is across the road about twenty feet. I grab hold of Mama's hand. "Mama, I have an idea. Instead of walking all the way to town, we can stop by the Clarks'. They're rich, so I think they have a telegraph machine. You can use it to send your message."

Not sure what she'll do when there's no such machine, but anything will be better than wandering through town. I steer her to the driveway and up the winding gravel drive. Oak trees at least a hundred years old mark the way and provide shade. At the end stands a large, white home that would impress even ole Mrs. Blake.

We climb six concrete steps to a porch so big our whole house could fit with room to spare. It winds around the front and both sides of the house, the kind of porch where children play chase and parents drink sweet tea.

I use the brass doorknocker and hold my breath, not sure what will happen next. The door opens to reveal a woman with a plate of cookies in one hand and a spatula in the other. An apron, belonging to a much smaller body, is cinched around her waist and stops short of covering rounded hips. A lilac cotton dress pulls tight across pillow like breasts, and dark eyes are set back into a face so black it shines.

"Yes?" When she smiles her cheeks look as if they have been stuffed with a few of the cookies.

"I'm Maggie and this is my mama, Elizabeth Wall. We stay in the house across the road, and we need to drop off the rent money."

"Come on in, I'm in the middle of baking Mr. Anthony his cookies. He just loves my oatmeal cookies. Folks have tried to get the recipe out of me for the last twenty years, but I won't tell. No sir, this recipe came from my mama's mama and I ain't about to let anyone know our secret."

She leads us past a huge winding staircase where I fight the urge to run up and slide down the banister. Instead, I hold on to Mama's arm and continue in the direction of fresh baked cookies.

"My name is Beatrice, but everyone calls me Bea. Been working here since I was fifteen years old. That's over twenty-five years. Land's sake, where does the time go?" She slides the last of the cookies onto the plate. "Now Maggie and Ms. Elizabeth, how about some cookies and milk?"

Before I can answer, Mama walks over to this dark skinned cookie baker. "I need to use your telegraph machine."

Bea looks from Mama to me and back again. "Telegraph machine?"

"I need to send a message to President Kennedy — it's a matter of life and death," Mama whispers.

"Lord have mercy, life or death?"

"Mama, why don't you sit down and have a cookie or two? The message can wait a few minutes," I say.

"No-o-o!" she howls. "It can't wait. Don't you understand they will kill me if I don't get this message to the president?" Mama's eyes dart back and forth so fast, I fear they'll pop out of her head.

I glance over at Bea now leaning against the strawberry papered wall. "What about a telephone? Can you call the president?" I ask. Mama needs to calm down before Bea falls out on the floor.

"The telephone is not safe! I need a telegraph machine!" Mama screams.

"Jesus, Lord," Bea mumbles.

"Do you have paper and pencil?" My face is on fire once again.

She nods, grabs a pad and pen from a drawer next to the sink and hands it to me. "Mama, look, you can write the message. Bea will take it to town and send the telegram. She'll get it there quicker than us because she's wearing flat shoes." Mama looks at Bea, who looks at me. I mouth the word 'please' and try not to cry.

"Yes ma'am, I can do that for you. I'll walk fast, too."

"You can't read the message. If you read the message they will kill you," Mama whispers.

Before Bea runs screaming from the room, I grab Mama and ease her down at the kitchen table. "Here, if you run out of paper, I'll get more."

Bea motions to follow her into a small room off the kitchen. I step into what looks like a small grocery store. Shelves from floor to ceiling are filled with any kind of food that comes in a can, sack, bag, or jar. We barely keep one small cabinet filled; rich folks need a whole room. I shake my head, all this for two old people.

"Should I call someone? What about your daddy?" she whispers.

The crazy mama's hard on folks that haven't dealt with this sort of thing before. Bless her heart; she was just trying to bake cookies.

"No, we don't need to call anyone. Soon as she writes her message, we'll be gone. Just throw the letter away."

"Are you sure she'll be all right?"

I nod.

Bea takes a deep breath as we walk back into the kitchen. The first page is complete and Mama is busy with the second. This will be a long message. I sigh and lean against the fireplace made from the same red bricks as the floor. Bea paces around the room ready to lock herself in the food closet if Mama does anything crazy.

When the scribbling stops, I walk over to the table. "Mama, you done?"

She folds the paper in half and sticks it out towards Bea.

"Yes ma'am, I'll take care of this for you." She grabs the letter, keeping a safe distance between herself and Mama.

"I'd appreciate you not mentioning this to anyone," I mumble.

"Sure, and Maggie, come back any time."

I notice the invitation doesn't include Mama. We walk out leaving Bea to stare at the secret message to President Kennedy.

❧

The mama I left home with and the mama beside me now, are two different women. Walking to the Clarks' was a woman chosen to save the president, the world, or maybe both. At this moment, she's a woman gripped with fear. Shallow, fast, breaths escape quivering lips no longer able to speak gibberish.

Her words are trapped inside with visions of cloaked communists on a mission of their own.

I steer Mama to the bedroom, unzip her dress and watch as she retreats under the covers in her slip. She looks small on the bed, more like a child than a mama. I crawl next to her, careful not to get too close, and stare at the ceiling. I move closer until the warmth of her body can be felt through the quilt. I wipe tears from her cheek.

"Mama, you did good. Bea will get the message sent, don't worry." When she is asleep I stand and watch the rise and fall of her chest. "Do you still see the bad men?" I whisper.

Suddenly, the need to leave this house pushes down so hard against my chest that I can do nothing but run. I go through the kitchen and living room, fly out the screen door and don't stop until the tree house ladder is within reach. When my hand touches the smooth wood, I breathe.

"Maggie, are you all right?"

I look up to see Sam's face peeping from the window. Her right eye, still swollen, has turned an ugly shade of purple. "Do you live in the tree house?" I climb the ladder and sit across from the window.

She smiles causing the eye to close. "Not yet, but that's not a bad idea. What's up? You don't look so good."

"Me? Have you looked in the mirror today? What have you done to take care of your eye? Really Samantha, you should see a doctor."

"I'm fine. Now, what's going on?"

I shrug and answer, "Just tired."

"Is it your mama?"

I cannot make myself lie and say she's fine. I can't pretend the new electrical treatments will be the cure we've prayed so many years for, and I'm unable to form the words *she'll be well soon*. Instead, I bury my face in my hands and sob.

Sam scoots across the plywood floor and drapes her arm around my shoulders. She doesn't say don't cry or that everything will be all right, she just pats and soothes with her hug.

When the tears stop, I lift my head. "Thanks."

"I'm your friend," she replies.

I want to ask where she learned to be a friend, and who taught her to love? It surely wasn't the drunk mama. I smile and say nothing.

"Mama came home drunk again. I got out of there this time."

"Maybe we could both move in here," I say.

"Yeah, until winter anyway or maybe your daddy could hook up a heater."

"We'll need a little stove and refrigerator," I add.

Sam giggles. "He might as well haul a bed up, and a tub would be nice."

"Why stop there? He could add on to make room for a sofa and radio."

Laughter spills out into the yard as we describe room after room of our new home. We don't stop until the tree house is larger than Mrs. Clark's plantation and includes a curved staircase with a banister large enough for two.

"Wouldn't it be great for us to live together?" she whispers.

I close my eyes and see a world with Sam, me, Daddy, and Mama all living together. A world free of drunk mamas and where crazy doesn't exist.

"You can stay with us anytime. Doesn't matter how long either," I say.

She stands. "I've got to go."

"Why don't you stay awhile? I'll fix us some lunch. We can eat right here in our soon-to-be home." I smile.

"Thanks, but I need to check on Mama. She was pretty bad off when she came in this morning. She'll need coffee and food."

I watch as Sam climbs down the ladder, jumps on her bike, and rides off to the drunk mama. "Lord, make her too tired to hit Sam." I say, loud enough for God to hear. "Can't you do something with the drunk mama? Not kill her or anything, just make her leave. Then, Sam can move in with us where she'll be safe. We'll be sisters. I'm sure you'll figure something out. Amen." ∼

⤙ NINE ⤚

I LEAVE THE TREE house long enough to grab a sandwich, Coke, a book on California, and Margaret Mitchell's *Gone With the Wind*. Even if our house goes up in flames, I will not come down until I finish reading the entire novel. The book has six hundred eighty-nine pages, so I'll be in the tree for a very long time.

Last summer, Mama read it in twelve days. She claims it's one of the best books ever written but not appropriate reading for an eleven year old girl. I open the book in an attempt to prove her wrong.

The first few pages go well, but by the time Scarlett promises to waltz with the Tarleton twins, I'm more interested in counting words than reading them. On page seven, there are five hundred ninety-three words. That fact alone makes it inappropriate for eleven year olds.

I leave Scarlett to worry about the Wilkes' party and travel to the beaches of California. Today I read about Santa Barbara.

Mountains, ocean, lots of people — maybe I'll live here. There's no Golden Gate Bridge, but Santa Barbara will do if I can't live in San Francisco. The sound of Daddy's truck pulls me back to Pearl. I poke my head out the window in time to see him climb from the cab. "Hey Daddy," I call.

He sees me and smiles. "What ya doing?"

"Reading. You're home early."

"No, it's 3:30."

It was eleven o'clock just a few minutes ago. Oh man, Mama hasn't had lunch. I jump from the third rung of the ladder and hit the ground running.

Daddy stops me by the clump of azalea bushes at the porch. "Where's the fire?"

"The time got away from me and I forgot to fix Mama's lunch." I look down at my bare feet. Somewhere in the distance, a bird sings a sad song. He's probably hungry too.

Daddy grabs my hand. "Maggie, that's all right, she can eat now. Where is she?"

"After the mission she went to bed," I answer.

"Mission?"

Fear is an emotion that has a voice all its own. Sometimes, it's quiet, just a whimper or moan, other times it's a cry in the middle of the night when a nightmare seems too real. Far too often, though, it's a scream while awake, when life becomes the nightmare. Today, it is wrapped up in one word.

"Everything's fine, Daddy. Mama had a message for President Kennedy. We walked over to the Clarks' to look for a telegraph machine. Their housekeeper convinced Mama to leave the message with her, said she would take it to town. Mama doesn't know there isn't a machine in Pearl. Anyway, she went to bed after that."

Daddy seems a few inches shorter as we walk into the living room. "Elizabeth, I'm home," he yells, "how about something to eat?"

Pink insulation clings to the bottom of his pants and socks when he slips off his boots. Must have been in an attic today. I grab a glass from the cabinet and fill it with water. Saw on television last week that a man in Shreveport died of heat stroke.

"Here Daddy, you need to drink some water. I'll bet you didn't drink any all day."

He takes the glass from my hand and sets it on the table. "Thanks, Mags, I'll drink it after I check on your Mama."

"You won't be around to check on her if you don't drink water," I mumble to myself. He's so busy taking care of Mama and me there's no time left for him. How long can a person do that before they just disappear?

"Maggie!"

I run to their room and find Daddy staring at an empty bed. Fear creeps up my spine, makes its way to my lungs, and sucks the air right out.

"Maggie, did you see her leave the house?" Daddy kneels on the floor and looks under the bed. "I need to know how much time she had to get away. Maggie, what time did you leave her?"

What time did I leave her? I didn't go to a friend's sleepover, or for a swim in a lake. There was no ice cream cone from Murray's, or new books from the library. I didn't leave her — I was in the front yard! I want to yell this, but a person has to breathe in order to scream. Right now, I'm fighting for air.

"We need to search the woods behind the house first." The words shake their way out of his mouth.

"Daddy, I ..."

"Sh-h-h," he says, finger across his lip.

I tilt my head and listen. At first there's only silence, but then I hear it — a soft, whimper coming from the closet. She's there, between black heels and brown loafers, knees pulled tight against her chest, staring into the dark.

Daddy sits on the floor. "Elizabeth, honey, why don't you come out of the closet? You're safe, nothing will harm you, I promise."

She doesn't stop him when he touches her arms and lifts her from the closet. He cradles and soothes, like a mother with a newborn baby, and eases her onto the bed. Daddy glances at the dresser coated with long, black hair. With a nod, he tells me to retrieve the scissors from the floor.

"Elizabeth, I'm going to even out your hair, then we'll get some dinner. There's left-over chicken. I'll mash some potatoes and slice some of the tomatoes from Milton's garden. You love fresh tomatoes."

Mama sits still and says nothing. As hair falls to the floor, I leave the room.

⚜

The only sound comes from a blue jay positioned between the porch and the tree house. Hidden from sight, his song is the only thing that lets the world know he exists. The cry of hunger from yesterday is replaced with a "maybe life ain't so bad" song this morning.

The swing glides back and forth as I glance down at the note in my hand. Mama couldn't wait; the electrical treatments will begin today. Years ago, I learned to ignore the words of doctors who claim to have just the right treatment. One of the crazier ones said she didn't get enough blood to her brain. For two days, she lay across my bed with her head hung off the side. Thought for sure it was going to burst from all the blood, but the skull remained intact; so did the voices.

Also, learned it doesn't do any good to get worked up about a treatment, no matter how smart the doctor. Mama's cures have mostly been medicines of all shapes and colors, none of which keeps her well long enough to be a real cure. Once a doctor claimed she just needed to be hypnotized. I've never been to medical school, but knew that deserved no hope at all. For some reason, though, I've decided to believe this new doctor and his treatment. Perhaps the cheery blue jay has brainwashed me, or I just need a change, but the electrical treatments sound promising.

It's time for something to work. I need Mama back, even for a few months, to brush my hair and say prayers at night; to climb in bed with me so we can read together for hours; to wake me up with a cup of coffee milk. I need her to see me when she looks into my eyes. ⌣

⟿ TEN ⟾

THE SOUND OF tires on gravel draws my gaze to the driveway. Sam, red hair hovering above her head, races toward the porch. She stops the bicycle just short of crashing into the azalea bushes.

"Is someone after you?" I ask.

She takes deep breaths, to slow her breathing so she can speak.

"You need some water?"

"No, I'm fine."

She's always fine. "What's up? Are you trying to break a record or something?"

Sam plops down on the swing. "Just wanted to see how fast I could go."

"Hey, you want to go to the Clarks'? The housekeeper may be baking cookies."

"No, I better not. Miss Clark calls me the spawn of Satan."

I lean in to get a closer look at her face. "Why in the world would she call you that?"

"It has to do with her husband. Mama and Mr. Clark use to be high school sweethearts. They even talked about gettin' married. Something happened and he broke it off with Mama and married ole Mary Anne. Guess all the land and money was just too good to pass up. Anyway, a few years ago Mr. Clark and Mama took up again. For a long time he came by our house a couple of times a week. Miss Clark was so busy with the family business she didn't even notice. Then one day, she found out and threatened to kick him out of her house. Money won again, and I say good riddance."

I stare at Sam. She talks as if the story was about her mama entering a cake at the state fair bake off.

"Maggie, you need to close your mouth before something flies in it," she says.

"Oh." I clamp my mouth shut and look at my feet.

"You think the cookies are good?"

"They smelled delicious."

"I reckon we could slip over for a few." She grins, and jumps off the swing. "Maybe the ole girl will be gone."

"She's probably at work, don't you think?" I run after Sam, who is half-way down the driveway. She walks as fast as she pedals.

"Yeah, she's probably at her sugar factory. That's where she spends most of her life."

"What about Mr. Clark, does he work?" I ask.

"He works there, too."

"How do you know so much?"

"Mama talks about them when she drinks." Sam kicks a rock in the air. It lands with a thud near the Clarks' driveway. She should be on a kick ball team.

"Do you know Bea?" I ask.

"I've seen her around."

I wait for more, but she only stares at the road. Lips drawn tight cause little lines to form around her mouth making her look like a broken old woman.

I change the subject. "Are you excited about going into seventh grade in September?"

"What's to be excited about?"

"We'll be in junior high. I've heard the seventh grade teachers are nice." I pretend we've just won a trip to San Francisco in order to sound enthusiastic.

"I hate school."

So much for enthusiasm. We walk up the drive without another word. The sweet smell of jasmine greets us as we get close to the porch. I close my eyes and take a deep breath. There's nothing better than the smell of jasmine or the flower off a magnolia tree. The last place we lived had a magnolia tree in the backyard. I pulled flowers off to keep in my pocket so I could smell them anytime I wanted.

A voice from the side of the house causes us to jump and bump into one another. We look to see Bea holding an empty wicker basket. "What have we here? You girls need something?" She glances around making sure we're alone.

"Just stopped by to visit. If you're busy, we can come back," I say.

"I was fixin' to get the cookies out the oven. Anyway, my tail's a-dragging, I could use a break. Come on round back."

I smile. "Are you by yourself?"

"They're at work, as usual. It's a shame to have this big house and never here to enjoy it. Afternoon Samantha."

"Hey," Sam answers.

"Today is chocolate chip day. Monday I bake oatmeal and Wednesday sugar. Mr. Anthony sure does love my cookies. I don't know who eats more of 'em, me or him. Miss Clark won't touch a single one. Says she doesn't want to get fat. Who ever heard of a cookie or two getting a person fat?"

I look at Bea's round face and expanding waist, but say nothing. We walk around the house past the clothesline, and enter a backyard filled with pecan trees. In the distance sits a wooden barn with ivy creeping up both sides. Tree-covered land goes on forever in all directions. She leads us to a screened porch, home to all sorts of flowers and plants. Two wicker chairs sit between a rubber plant tall as Sam, and a pot of yellow flowers. I could live right here on this porch and be happy as fish in the Pacific Ocean.

"Come on in, girls. My nose says the cookies are ready to eat."

We follow her into a small room with three pair of rubber boots neatly standing under a row of coats. She opens a closet with shelves of gardening tools, places the basket on the floor, and leads us to the kitchen. "Have a seat at the table while I get the cookies."

"Thanks," I say.

Sam rubs the bottom of her plaid shirt, eyes darting from the fancy table to the brick fireplace. The only place she'd be more uncomfortable is the Baptist church on Sunday morning.

"Hope we're not bothering you," I say.

"No, it's nice to have company now and again. I'm done with the cleaning; all that's left is supper."

"You cook for them too?" Sam's eyes are wide as the saucers holding our cookies.

Bea chuckles and nods her head. "Honey, I do everything there is to do around this house. Today, it's jambalaya, greens and cracklin' bread." She places the plates and glasses on the table. "Now, eat up and enjoy."

"What about you? Are you going to eat some cookies?" I slide the plate closer and take a gulp of milk.

"I'm as full as a tick. Can't help but eat the dough when I make cookies. So, what are y'all doing this fine summer day?"

Sam shrugs and continues shoving cookies in her mouth.

"No plans," I say.

"No plans? Thought girls your ages would be busy as bees. Don't y'all go to sleepovers and talk about boys?"

"I've never been invited to a sleepover," I say.

Sam stops munching long enough to answer, "Wouldn't go if I was invited."

"That so?" Bea rubs her chin with a dry, wrinkled hand. "How would you two like a tour of the house?"

"Sure," I answer.

Sam grabs two cookies from the plate and we follow Bea out of the kitchen. She plays tour guide as we make our way on wood floors so polished I can just about see myself. "That there is Miss. Clark's office. She keeps the door locked, not even Mr. Anthony has a key. Across there is the sitting room. She only opens that door when company comes. The den is at the end of the hall and this here's the dining room. Let me warn you," Bea says, "Miss Clark remodeled the dining room and a few other rooms in the house. She made 'em different colors. The dining room is now the green room. She claims green is good for the digestive system. Sounds kind of crazy to me, but then, what do I know?" She winks and opens the double doors.

I scan the room. Walls and tablecloth the color of clover, deep green velvet drapes from ceiling to floor, and a rug with different shades of green swirls make me wonder if we've somehow made it outside. "She shouldn't have any trouble digesting her food."

Bea laughs as we walk around a shiny brown table like the one we used to have.

"Who all eats here?" Sam asks.

"Mostly, just the two of them. Sometimes they have company over, but not often. When I was a kid, Miss Sarah, Miss Clark's mama, had parties all the time. The ladies would arrive in all their finery, hair put up with feathers and jeweled pins; the men dressed in suits and hats looking just as good as the ladies. Those folks would eat and drink till all hours of the morning. Yes sir, Miss Sarah sure could throw a fine shindig. Couldn't of asked for a better boss lady. It was a sad day when Miss Sarah passed. Hasn't been the same around here since."

"Do you live here?"

"I stay in a room off the back porch. When Mama was alive we lived in a house out back, but when she died, Miss Sarah thought it best for me to live in the big house. Been here ever since. Let me go get the cookies and milk. We can eat in here." Before we can answer, she heads for the kitchen, lilac skirt swishing with each step.

"Can you imagine the parties they had here?" I ask. Visions of dinner guests, men dressed in dark suits and women in white gloves and dresses that reach the floor, swirl around my head. "Wonder where Miss Sarah's guests came from?"

Sam rubs her hand along the top of the table. "Must of imported 'em because I've never seen women in Pearl with feathers and jeweled pins in their hair, and there's only one or two men who own suits."

I laugh. "One day we'll go to a party like that. You know, get all dressed up and dance all night."

"Yeah, right," Sam says.

"Wouldn't it be fun to wear long dresses and fix ourselves up like the girls in *Life* magazine?"

Before Sam can explain why that wouldn't be any fun at all, Bea swishes in carrying a silver tray of milk and cookies. We sit at one end of the table and begin stuffing chocolate chip cookies in our mouths.

"There won't be any left for Mr. Anthony," I say between bites.

"Don't you worry, I can always bake more."

Sam's mouth opens to speak when the front door slams shut. She looks ready to bolt until a man's voice calls for Bea.

"We're in the dining room. What you doing home this time a day? Are you sick?" she calls.

"No, I forgot some contracts we need for a meeting this afternoon. Mary Anne threw a good one. I'm going to need a few of your cookies to get me through the day." Mr. Anthony laughs. "I also need . . ." He stops in the doorway as if running into the Great Wall of China.

"Mr. Anthony, this here is Maggie. Her family rents your house across the street."

He nods in my direction, but doesn't take his eyes off Sam. She stares back with the same blue eyes.

"You know Samantha," Bea says.

"How are you?" he asks.

Looking down at the table, Sam mumbles, "Fine."

Mr. Anthony does not look at all like the man I imagined. For one thing, he has a frame belonging to a much younger man, not one that eats hundreds of cookies. Dark hair slicked back shows no signs of gray and very few wrinkles line his face. Black suit, starched white shirt and blue tie along with smooth hands speak of days spent in an office.

"Are you enjoying the break from school?" he asks.

She looks at him until her eyes fill with tears. I stare at her with my mouth open. Sam has never shed a tear in my presence, not even when the drunk mama beat her, but now she's on the verge of wailing from two simple questions.

"We just stopped by to visit Bea," I say. "She gave us some cookies, hope you don't mind."

He looks at me for the first time. "No, not at all, eat as many as you want. In fact, take some home with you. Afterwards, why don't you two go to Murray's for ice cream? Would you like that Samantha?" He digs money from his pocket.

"I don't need your money." She stands and walks out the room. The sound of the front door slamming echoes through the dining room.

When it's clear Mr. Anthony and Bea can't think of a single word to say, I stand. "Well, I'd better go." My eyes stay on the five-dollar bill still stuck out in my direction. A banana split sure would be good. I wrap the left over cookies in a napkin, then shove my free hand in the pocket of my jeans. Don't want to accidentally grab the money. "Thanks for the cookies. It was nice to meet you Mr. Anthony." I turn to leave.

"Maggie, will you let me know if Samantha needs anything?" he asks.

"She's fine," I say without looking back.

I find Sam in the tree house, knees crunched to her chest, face wet from tears. I slide over and put my arm around her shoulder.

"I lied," she says.

"What do you mean?"

"I didn't want him to stop coming around. He would sit and talk, ya know, really talk to me, and listened to what I said, like it was important. Mama cooked dinner for him and we ate at the table like a family. We were able to live in a good part of town, and always had electricity and water. We even had a telephone. I pretended he was Mama's husband. Silly, huh?"

"No Sam, that's not silly."

We sit and stare at nothing for a long time. Don't know why life has to be so hard. Mama says God uses the bad times to build strength. Wonder how strong a person needs to be before things get easier.

"Thanks, Maggie. I'm fine now," she says. "Guess I better head home."

"Hey, I've got an idea. Let's have a sleepover. Go get your clothes and come back. We can stay up all night and talk about boys."

"Boys?" She crinkles her nose as if a bad smell just swept through the tree house.

"Isn't that what you're supposed to talk about at slee-povers?" I ask.

"I'll bring my marbles and you get the cards. That'll be better than talking about boys."

"Yeah, that sounds good. See ya in a couple of hours." ⤳

⤙ ELEVEN ⤚

FIRST THING I do is make my bed, because an unmade bed has to be unacceptable at a sleepover. Next, I make Mama's peanut butter and jelly sandwiches; the ones with no crusts that are made when she's in the mood for a party. I slice each sandwich into four squares, and cover the plate with a clean, damp dishrag. Sweet tea is in the refrigerator, potato chips and crackers on the counter. Something chocolate would be nice, but the last cookies were eaten before I knew about the sleepover. Maybe Daddy will think of some more food. I dig the cards from the drawer and stick them on the table.

Inspections of the food, several walks through each room to make sure everything is neat, and waiting on the porch swing fill the next two hours. Daddy arrives before Sam. I meet him at the truck.

"How's Mama?"

"She'll be fine." He slams the truck door and gives me a quick hug. "How was your day?"

"I'm having a sleepover tonight."

"Girls from school coming?"

"Sam's the only one. Thought I should start small, this being my first sleepover and all."

"Think that's a good idea. You need to get the hang of it before going big." Daddy switches his metal lunch box to his left hand, puts his right arm around my shoulder and guides me inside the house.

"I made party sandwiches, and we have tea and chips. Do you think that's enough snacks? We're out of cookies, but I can make chocolate milk. What else do people eat at sleepovers?" I open the refrigerator and search for anything made with large amounts of sugar.

"I'm not sure. Milton's wife sent over some chicken and dumplings yesterday. You can have that for supper."

"Yeah, but what about party food? Do we need more?"

Daddy closes the refrigerator door. "How 'bout I take you both to Murray's for ice cream after dinner? Unless sundaes aren't considered party food."

"That would be great." I grab him around the waist and squeeze.

"It's your summer break; you've got to have at least one chocolate sundae before school starts up again." He reaches down and brushes bangs out of my eyes. "Maggie, you're gonna be blind soon if you don't cut these bangs."

I grin and change the subject. "Sam's bringing her marbles and I've got the cards out. Maybe we can catch fireflies."

From the kitchen chair, Daddy begins the shedding of work routine. This time no pink insulation clings to his socks; no attic job today. His hands shake, just for a second, as he unlaces the boots.

"Daddy, did you eat today? What about water? You know people drop dead right in their tracks from not drinking water. Did you know that? Really Daddy, you've got to take better care of yourself. What would Mama and me do if something happened …" Suddenly my throat is so tight no words can make their way out.

"Maggie, don't worry, nothing's going to happen to me. Really, honey, I'm fine." Daddy smiles to back up his words, but I know it's his pretend smile. I've seen it a thousand times. It's the one he used after Mama took a bottle of pills and we ran into a neighbor in the emergency room. The one he gave to the ladies from church when they promised to visit Mama even though we both knew they wouldn't be caught dead at the state mental hospital. Today, it's the same smile I saw when he assured me the move to Pearl was just what Mama needed.

I turn and leave the room. "Well, I can't follow you around with a jug of water," I say slamming my bedroom door.

I pick up the photograph of the Golden Gate Bridge, plop down on the edge of the bed and let out a moan that should come from a dying animal. I wish someone would tell the truth. If anyone would admit that even on a good day life is hard; or sometimes no matter how loud you pray God just doesn't seem to hear, well, I'd fall out on the floor. Then, when the shock left my body, I'd get up and do a dance.

Daddy comes in without a knock. "Maggie, I don't want you to worry about me. You need to enjoy being a kid for once."

"I'm not a kid. I'll be twelve in less than two months. You do realize that I'm almost in high school."

"Aren't you going into seventh grade?"

"Yeah, but in just two years I'll be in high school."

He leans against the wall and runs his hands through his hair. "I swear Maggie; you were born an old lady."

"An old lady? That's as bad as being called a kid!"

"I didn't mean it like that," he moans. "It's just that ever since you were little you've been taking care of everyone. I just want you to enjoy life. You know, make friends and have a little fun."

I don't have the heart to tell him moving every couple of years adds an additional challenge to making friends, especially in a place like Pearl. All the kids have been together since first grade. It will be high school before I'm not the new kid, that is, if we're still here.

"I am having a sleepover tonight," I mumble.

"Yeah, that's great. I want you to do more things that girls your age are doing. Ya know, sleepovers, and, whatever else girls your age do."

I shrug. "I don't know what they do."

"That's the point. You should know."

"Daddy, I'm fine." The words creep out without my permission. Maybe it's a disease we all have. "Sam's my friend and we do have fun. Today we were over at the Clarks' having cookies with Bea."

"Is Bea their daughter?" Hope spills off each word.

"No, their housekeeper."

"Housekeeper? How old is she?"

"Well, older than you, but she's fun. Said we can go over anytime."

Daddy shakes his head. "That's not exactly what I had in mind when I said to have fun."

I grab his hand and pull until he sits beside me on the bed. Dark, coarse hair has sprouted on his face, and he needs a haircut in the worse way. Stains blended together make it impossible to know the color of his work shirt. If I saw him on the street, and he wasn't my Daddy I'd cross to the other side.

"You don't need to worry about me. Honestly, have you looked in the mirror lately?" I reach up and rub the stubble on his face.

"Yeah, I need to shave," he says.

"You also need a haircut, and please wash that shirt."

He laughs for the first time in days. "There you go again, taking care of me."

"Well, someone has to. Look what happens in just a couple of days — you fall apart."

"Maggie …"

"Just kidding, Daddy. Don't worry about me, really I'm fine." What is it with those words? They're taking over the world.

"Will you promise to enjoy this summer," Daddy asks.

"Yeah, I promise." I look into his eyes and pray for truth. "How's Mama?"

He looks from me to the floor. "She's, well, today was hard."

It may just be time for that dance. "What happened?"

He stands and walks to the door, "It was just hard to leave her. She'll be fine though. Want some dinner?"

My eyes go back to the photograph in my hand. "No, I'll wait for Sam."

⚜

The last thing I remember is curling up on the porch swing to wait for Sam. Now, I'm in bed, alone. As the quilt falls to the floor, I discover I'm still dressed in the pedal pushers and pink blouse from yesterday. Even though it happened by accident, Daddy may be on to something. Wearing clothes to bed saves time in the morning, and there would be fewer clothes to wash. I run a comb through my straight-as-a-board hair and head for the kitchen. The party sandwiches are in the refrigerator, still wrapped in the dishrag. I slip one of the crustless delights from under the cloth, stuff it in my mouth, and before it reaches my stomach, know what must be done.

I've always tried hard to listen to Daddy. He doesn't make up a bunch of rules just because he can, so it's easy to follow the few he does make. This time, though, I just can't obey. I have to find out why Sam never made it over. Pictures of a bruised and swollen face fill my mind as I pedal down Clark Road.

Don't know what makes people do the things they do. What makes a mama get drunk and beat her own flesh and blood? Is it the same thing that causes a mama's mind to get so confused being electrocuted is her only hope? Reckon those two belong in my book for unanswered questions. They'll be right next to the one about how Noah got all those animals in the ark. Mama says some things aren't meant to be revealed until we get to heaven. Sure hope God has a lot of free time. If I left earth at this very moment, I'd take a couple of hundred unanswered questions to heaven.

Some folks go through life without any. They take whatever comes their way with a nod. Maybe that's easier, maybe questions just make life more difficult. If that's true, my life is destined to be hard, because I can't seem to stop asking 'em. There are just too many things that make no sense at all. Wish I was more like the well Mama. She has a faith so big it covers over all her questions and fills her with a peace so huge it oozes out and splashes everyone that comes her way.

I cross Thompson Creek and think of the only time she questioned why. It was last summer in Minden while on one of our many adventures. We were headed for a pond in the back of someone's property. Someone we didn't know.

"Mama, are you sure we should cross over their fence?" I asked.
Mama smiled as she pushed the barbed wire down for me to climb over. "I'm sure they won't mind. Come on Mags, it'll be fun. I heard there's a pond back here."

A forest of trees was between us and the brown farmhouse, so unless they were fishing at their pond, there wasn't much chance we'd be seen. We followed a path through the woods for a mile or so, with nonstop talk from Mama about how beautiful everything was: beautiful trees, beautiful flowers, beautiful, beautiful, beautiful. I walked and listened to her voice.

"There it is, Mags, there's the pond." Mama laughed. "Come on, bet I can beat you."

A pond, the size of our front yard, sat in a field just outside the thick trees. Mama took off and didn't stop until she fell on the soft ground next to the muddy water. I joined her, so close our legs touched. The only sound was the in and out of our breath as we sucked in air. It wasn't until our lungs ceased to burn and the movement of our chest slowed that she spoke.

"Isn't this a perfect day?"

"Yep," I answered, eyes closed.

"I'm so thankful for days like today." She was quiet for awhile, then whispered, "Maggie, do you think my sickness is a punishment from God?"

I grew up with an unspoken rule: no discussion of the illness when Mama was well. We didn't want to give more than it already took. I sat up and looked down at cheeks still flushed from our run, and lips with just a hint of the red lipstick applied that morning. Blue eyes met mine and I knew this was an important question.

"Why would God be mad at you?" I asked.

"When I was a girl, I felt God wanted me to be a missionary, you know, go to China or somewhere." Mama closed her eyes. "I didn't listen, so maybe God is mad."

I wished we were with a preacher or even a Sunday School teacher, anyone that was an expert on God, but of course those folks are never anywhere to be found when you need them. I didn't speak for a long time, hoping God would send one of his angels to talk with Mama. When no one arrived, I took a deep breath and answered the best way I could.

"You know how preachers talk about God being our heavenly father? Well, that makes me think of Daddy. Sometimes I do things Daddy doesn't want me to do, but he doesn't get mad. He's punished me before, but never for long. I figure God is better at being a father than Daddy. Mama, I don't think God is still punishing you for something that long ago. I mean, I've never heard a preacher say that God holds grudges."

Mama laughed then, a laugh that began deep in her belly. She wrapped her arms around her stomach as tears slid down her face. "Maggie, I swear, you make more sense than most psychiatrists I know."

"Mama that log out there has more sense than your doctor."

This time, we both laughed, until the ache in our bellies was so bad we had to stop.

"Don't ever forget how to laugh, Maggie. No matter what, don't lose your sense of humor," she said. "Now, how about a swim?"

"We don't have our swimming clothes."

Before I could stand, Mama kicked off her shoes and jumped in the pond, clothes and all. ❧

~(TWELVE)~

THE MOMENT I cross the tracks on the way to Samantha's I know this is a different Pearl. Gone are the white picket fences and yards scattered with impatiens and day lilies. There are no mamas on porch swings singing choruses of "hello" and "how are you?" to neighbors. There are no children crowding the sidewalks with their bikes. In fact, there are no sidewalks.

Sam's house is six down from the tracks, across the street from a bar room, which is probably why the drunk mama picked it. She surely didn't move in because of its beauty. Most of the paint has long since fallen off the wood frame, the screen door is gone, and there's not a curtain in sight. If a house can feel, this one's depressed. I make my way through the tall grass to the front steps.

"Maggie, what you doing here?"

I turn to see Sam walk from the side of the house. Her eyes are swollen and red from crying. I walk over to her. "I waited for you last night."

"Yeah, she wouldn't let me leave. She has company coming and needed me to clean the house."

"Oh," I say.

"Hey, you want to see something?" She pulls a small purple marble out of her pocket.

"That's a beauty." I smile.

"You can have it." She puts the marble in my hand.

"No, Sam, this is yours."

"You keep it, Maggie. Anyway, I've got plenty more. Keep 'em buried in the backyard."

My mouth is wide open again. "Why do you bury your marbles?"

"Keeps 'em safe," she says.

I don't ask safe from what, just nod my head like the ground is a great place to keep marbles.

"I've got a beautiful tiger eye. Let me go get it."

Before I can stop her, she disappears around the side of the house. Sam needs to get away from this place before she decides to bury herself back there. I walk to the front of the house and sit on the one step that isn't cracked.

"Samantha, girl, you better get in here," a voice calls from inside.

"She's in the back," I yell.

The door opens and the drunk mama walks out on the porch. A face with the same full lips and pointed chin as Sam stares down at me; the same red curls snake down her back and scream for a brush. The only difference between the two is their eyes. Sam's are the color of the sky on a clear summer day; the drunk mama's are dark brown, almost black, and are like looking in an empty hole.

"Who are you?" She reaches in the pocket of her robe and pulls out a pack of cigarettes.

"Maggie Wall, I'm a friend of Sam's."

The drunk mama stares at me while she lights a cigarette. She blows smoke in my direction. "Tell your lazy friend to get inside. She has work to finish."

"Sam isn't lazy." The words are out of my mouth before I can stop them.

The drunk mama takes another draw on her cigarette. "Yeah, and she's not stupid either."

"Sam has more sense than most people I know." My face feels hot.

She turns to go back inside. "You must know some real dumb people."

"She's comin' to stay at my house for a few days," I say barely above a whisper.

The drunk mama wheels around and gives me a look that makes me doubt my intelligence. She throws the cigarette down and stomps it with a slipper-clad foot. I wait for the slap that's sure to come. "Who do you think you are telling me what my daughter's gonna do?" she hisses.

"Someone that knows what you do to her and will tell the sheriff if it doesn't stop."

The drunk mama laughs. "Do you think the sheriff cares what happens to Sam? The sheriff, like everyone else in this town, is too good to worry about people like us."

"Well, I know one person that cares about her — Mr. Anthony Clark." This takes the smile right off her face. The words have punched her hard in the stomach, and the look of pain brings me great joy.

"You sure are a conniving little thing." She walks inside and slams the door.

I push my hands into my pockets. Conniving makes them shake. ❧

~ THIRTEEN ~

IT'S THE THIRD day for Sam to be at our house. She sits, dressed in my tan pants and yellow-flowered blouse, between Daddy and me at the kitchen table. He deals five cards to each of us.

Sam looks at her cards and lets out a loud whistle. "Mr. Frank, this is the best hand yet. I don't need a single card."

"You're not supposed to tell when you have a good hand." I look at my cards and shake my head. "I'm out."

"Come on Maggie, don't go out," she pleads.

"I've got nothing."

"What about you Mr. Frank?" Sam's grin spreads across her face like a kid on Christmas morning.

Daddy looks at his cards and throws in two matchsticks. "I'm in."

She pushes four sticks to the middle of the table. "I raise you two."

"This is against my better judgment, but here goes." He adds two more matchsticks to the pile. "Now, I call." Sam turns over an ace, king, queen, jack, ten and nine. "A royal flush, well, I can't beat that. That's your third win in a row. I swear, girl, you sure did catch on to poker quick."

She giggles, adding her winnings to the fifty or so sticks neatly stacked on the table. "Want to play again?"

Poker is all we've played since Daddy taught us the game Saturday night. It's a fun game, but not fun enough to play three days straight. I haven't complained though, and will play for three more days if that's what Sam wants. She hasn't stopped smiling since we began.

"I could sit here all evening, but supper won't cook itself." Daddy pushes his cards to the center of the table and stands. "What y'all hungry for?"

I smile and say, "Steak, baked potato and chocolate cake."

Daddy grabs a box from the cabinet. "What about left over meat loaf and instant mashed potatoes? We may have a couple of chocolate moon pies left."

"Please let me make the potatoes. Last time you fixed it we had to drink 'em."

He laughs and shoves the box my way. "I could have sworn the directions said two cups of water."

"Sam, you want to help?" I ask.

"I should be going home, tomorrow's grocery day." She's no longer smiling.

Daddy brushes his hand along the top of her head. "Eat dinner before you head home. I'm betting Maggie's potatoes won't be any better than mine."

"I don't know, Mr. Frank, yours were like soup." Sam grins. "What ya want me to do?"

"Just sit there and entertain us while we cook. Tell us about yourself. You've lived here all your life?"

"Yes sir," Sam says.

Daddy pours a can of corn into a pot on the stove. "You have family here?"

"No, it's just me and mama." She folds and unfolds her hands.

"Tell us something about Pearl," I say, anxious to know any bit of information that will make the town interesting. I mean New York brags about the Empire State Building and San Francisco has the Golden Gate Bridge. The only thing Pearl has is oak trees, and may just be the smallest town in the world. The welcome sign boasts a population of 894 folks, must be 897 now that we've moved here.

"Like what?"

I reread the directions, pour water into the pot and answer, "Anything."

Sam leans forward. "Well, the president of the bank ran off with his secretary last year. They up and left in the middle of the night."

Make that a population of 895.

Daddy clears his throat. "What about Murray's? Isn't that the oldest building in town?"

Sam takes a deep breath. "Think so. When I was in fourth grade, Doc took over after his daddy died. He's not a real doctor, but he went to school in Mississippi to learn about medicine. They added the drugstore in the back when he finished school. Doc's engaged to Annabelle Whitney, the librarian, but I doubt they'll ever get married."

Just the mention of Doc's name gets my face to burning. "Why you think that?"

"Well, folks say he's been in love with Carol Anne since high school. He's at Sunshine every chance he gets. The other day he was in there his whole lunch hour, hanging on every word out of her mouth. I give his engagement two months."

Not sure where Sam gets her information, but it makes sense. Why else would someone like Doc hang out at Sunshine?

In only minutes, I'm ready to run from the store screaming. An entire novel can be read while waiting in the checkout line. One day, I had to put a gallon of ice cream back in the freezer three times so it wouldn't melt. Doesn't matter how many people are in line either, Carol Anne talks to each and every one as if there's not another soul in the store. She questions them about their children, their health, even how their pets are doing. The last time I was there, a man talked for fifteen minutes solid about his horse.

Strange thing is people don't seem to mind. While waiting their turn with Carol Anne, they talk to each other about quilting, or the latest gospel sing, or some other exciting part of their lives. Having their business broadcasted to all the shoppers doesn't bother them one bit, either. In fact, they seem to live for the opportunity. I, on the other hand, am a disappointment to all. I wait in line without uttering a single word, answer Carol Anne's questions with nods and grunts, and walk from the store wondering what I've done to deserve this town.

"Samantha, why don't you set the table?" Daddy says, ending an extremely interesting discussion.

When the food's gone and the dishes washed, Sam walks to the front door. "Thanks for the sleepover."

Daddy pushes open the screen. "Samantha, come anytime and stay as long as you like."

Sam throws her arms around Daddy. He hugs back and gives me a smile. It only took him a day to win her over. Daddy has a way of filling the empty spots in folks.

"Thanks, Mr. Frank."

"Maybe you can come back tomorrow after you shop," I suggest.

"Yeah, maybe," she says.

My stomach aches as I watch Sam climb on her bike and pedal away. I close my eyes and see the drunk mama trip over her robe, crash to the floor and crack her head open. She's rushed to the hospital, but too much alcohol soaked blood has seeped from the huge crack. The men from the funeral home bury her by Sam's marbles. After the funeral, that only Mr. Anthony attends, Sam moves in with us and we all live happily ever after.

Mama would not be pleased with these thoughts. She would, in fact, be horrified. I've lost count of the times she has said we should never hate another human being. Actually, the absence of hate is not enough for Mama. According to her, every person on earth needs to be loved because God loves them. I've tested her many times, and she never sways from her belief, but then, she hasn't met the drunk mama. ❧

~(FOURTEEN)~

BY THE MIDDLE of June a routine emerges that has the feel of a comfortable, pair of worn shoes. Daddy comes home from work to find Sam and me with cards or a book in our hands. The three of us throw together dinner, then its poker, hearts or some other card game. Wednesday nights we watch the Dick Van Dyke Show, and eat moon pies. Sam sleeps over two or three nights a week, and there's been no trouble from the drunk mama since the mention of Mr. Anthony's name.

Today, like most days when Sam's not around, I'm following Bea around the Clarks' plantation. "What they got you doing today?" I ask.

She mops her face with a red handkerchief and places the empty clothesbasket on the back porch. "Fixin' to shell some butter beans."

"I'll help."

She motions toward the wooden rocker next to her stool. "No child, this ain't no job for a young lady like yourself. Just sit and keep me company." Fingers move quickly pushing beans from their shells. "Won't take me long, then I'll fix us some lemonade. Made it fresh this morning."

I grab a bean from the bowl in Bea's lap. "Just want to try." Before the shell is opened, it wiggles out of my hand and lands on the floor.

She hands me a wooden bowl. "Try again."

Two more land by my feet before I manage to separate the bean from the shell. "You like working here?" I ask.

"Don't know nothing else. Been coming here since I was a baby. Mama worked here and brought me along. Miss Sarah read books to me while Mama did her work. She was the kindest white lady I ever met. Taught me to read and do numbers. It was a sad day when she passed."

"When did you start working here?"

"When I was fifteen Mama got the sugar and died not long after."

"Sorry your mama died," I say, not sure how sugar kills a person.

"Yeah, well, we all gonna die of something. Anyway, that's when I took over."

"Bet you've seen lots of stuff happen around here." I grab another bean. "Do you know Sam's mama?"

"This is a small town. Why you ask?"

"Thought you may know about her since you work for Mr. Anthony."

Bea's fingers stop for a moment. "My mama taught me to be like the old lady who fell out the wagon." She glances my way and laughs. "Means if you ain't in something don't get involved."

"Well, what if you're in it, kind of?"

"Then, you gotta do what you can." She takes the bowl from my hand. "But Maggie, be careful. Folks can be mighty mean when you meddle in their lives."

"Some people are mean even when you don't meddle," I say.

"Come on, child, time for a break."

We walk into the kitchen and Bea pours two glasses of lemonade. She leans against the counter and takes a sip. "Did you hear about those bandits escaping prison over in San Francisco?"

"No," I say between gulps.

"Mr. Clark was talking about it this morning. These three men dug their way out with spoons. Wouldn't have believed it if someone else had told me, but Mr. Clark swears it's the truth. Yes sir, they dug themselves right out then jumped in the bay and swam all the way to land. The FBI is looking for 'em this very minute."

"Was it Alcatraz?"

"Think so, yes that's what he said."

"Must have taken them months to dig through rock." I place the empty glass on the counter. "Better go, it's almost time for Daddy to get off work."

I walk home and for the next week think of nothing else but the spoon-digging convicts.

∽✠∾

For the first time since Mama was put in Wakefield, my mind is not occupied with stories or cards. Today, I want nothing more than to be alone with my memories. I'm in Mama's room digging through the dresser drawer. My hands search through cotton panties and silk stockings, finding what I need folded neatly at the bottom. I remove the slip from the drawer, pull it over my head, and watch as it falls to the floor. Next, I reach for the thing that is always needed when she's been gone this long — her crystal perfume bottle. I bring it close to my neck, close my eyes, pressing the bulb until I'm embraced by her scent. With eyes still closed I crawl under the state quilt. I drink in the smell of honeysuckle on my skin and think of her, pushing through visions of crazy to find the well Mama.

⚭

"Maggie, honey, I got the most wonderful books from the library."

She sat down beside me on my bed where I was drawing another masterpiece. Half a tablet of discards were scattered around the room. Mama smiled with lips the color of rubies. The day before, they were pink, compliments of the make-up counter at the Five and Dime. A picture of the latest short hair styles taped to the refrigerator went up the beginning of the week. So far, there was only courage enough for bright lips.

"What are you drawing?" she asked.

"I'm trying to draw a boy and his dog. So far it looks more like an alien and his space creature. I'm really terrible at this."

Mama picked up the tablet. "I can make out the dog's tail."

I laughed. "That's the boy's leg. Like I said, I'm no artist."

"There are all types of artists, not just the ones who draw. I could teach you how to make a collage," she said.

"Yeah?" I crumbled the alien picture into a ball, watched it sail across the room and bounce off the wall. "I'm bound to be better at gluing pictures, than drawing 'em."

"First, let's read. Your bed or outside?" She gathered the books in her arms and stood.

I scooted back on the bed and answered, "Here." We positioned our pillows against the headboard so they formed the perfect support. "Mama, before we read, will you tell me one of your stories?"

"Sure, Mags, which one?"

She scooted close and raised her arm. I leaned in, resting in the curve of her body. She smelled of rain on a warm summer's night, and for that moment was a regular mama. "You decide," I said.

"All right, I'll tell you about the most wonderful day of my life. It was exactly one o'clock in the morning. I was exhausted, but couldn't sleep because I was waiting for the nurse. She finally appeared carrying a small bundle. She tucked a blanket the color of a bouquet of bright pink carnations in my arms and left me to hold the most beautiful baby ever born. You looked up at me with these amazing green eyes and seemed to know exactly who I was. From your small round head, to your ten little toes, you were perfect."

"Where was Daddy?" I asked, already knowing the answer.

"He was in the corner of the room sound asleep. I wanted you all to myself, so I let him sleep." She kissed the top of my head and continued. "As you lay in my arms I knew you were the best thing to ever happen in this life."

"Did Daddy wake up then?"

"Yes, he took you in his arms and cried."

I squeezed her hand and whispered, "Mama, you're the best mama in the whole world." I looked up and found tears running down her face.

The sound of Daddy's truck draws me back. Jumping up, I yank the slip over my head and stuff it back into its home. My heart races as I head to the front door.

"Daddy, what's wrong? Why are you home in the middle of the afternoon?"

He walks in and kisses the top of my head. "Your mama's coming home."

"Today?"

Daddy walks through the living room still wearing his work boots. "Yep, I'm going to get her as soon as I change clothes. Met with the doctor at lunch and he said the shock treatments were a success. She'll have to stay on her medicine, of course, but he has high hopes." He disappears down the hall.

"High hopes," I repeat slowly, letting the words sink into my brain. Not just plain hope or a little hope, but high hope. A smile creeps across my face as I run to the closet. I pull out tennis shoes, black loafers, books, and clothes that have somehow never made it to the hangers. The sign is in the back corner. The cardboard, wrinkled and torn around the edges, still clearly displays its red marker message of Welcome Home Mama. I find the tape hidden inside my church shoes and cram everything back in the closet. "This place is getting down right dangerous," I say aloud.

"Maggie, I'm going. Be back in a while." He slams the door and is gone.

❧

When she steps from the truck, I am there. Arms go around her waist and pull tight. She's home.

"Maggie, why don't we let your mama get inside? Get out of this heat."

"Oh, sorry, Mama, come on, I made some sweet tea. Would you like some?" I grab her hand and lead the way to the house. "Also made grilled cheese, but Daddy could make his pancakes with butter and syrup, if you'd rather have that. Couldn't you Daddy?"

He laughs and opens the screen door. "Sure, I can do that."

I still have her hand as we walk to their bedroom. I motion to the sign hanging slightly crooked over the bed. "You still like it?"

She mumbles a reply as Daddy slips the suitcase on the bed. Dresses go in the closet, underclothes in the dresser, and tooth-brush in the blue glass next to the bathroom sink. Mama drops my hand and moves toward the bed.

"Elizabeth, are you hungry?"

"No, would it be all right if I rest awhile?" Her mouth forms a smile.

Daddy pulls the quilt back and she climbs into bed still in a pale blue dress that hangs loosely on her body. "We'll have dinner later."

When we are in the kitchen I say, "She looks pale."

"She'll be fine."

"She's too quiet."

"She's always quiet at first."

This is true, but I want this time to be different. "Yeah, she'll be fine," I say. ⌣

⤛ FIFTEEN ⤜

THIS MORNING I find Mama on the porch swing. She doesn't hear the door open, so I watch for a while. I wish for a camera, to save the way she looks as she pushes the swing back and forth with bare feet, the way she holds the coffee cup in both hands, head titled to one side, and stares into the yard.

Mama always changes something about herself when she gets home from the hospital. This time, a box of Clairol has added touches of red to hair that is now much shorter. In fact, it's just a little longer than the chin-length style of Jackie Kennedy. The First Lady's picture, cut from *Life* magazine, stayed taped to the refrigerator most of last year while Mama tried to get the courage to cut off her hair. Now, only soft curls come between her and the style in the picture.

She's been home two weeks. Daddy says each passing day brings her closer to the Elizabeth he married, the one before the sickness; and I can't remember a time she's been better.

For the first time in a long time, we've got ourselves some high hopes. I shift my weight making a board creak.

She looks my way. "Maggie, how long have you been there? I didn't even hear you. Come sit with me."

I sit beside her and she gives me a sip of coffee. It's bitter and cold, but I drink it anyway. She moves the swing again and looks past the dogwood in the yard. "Morning is my favorite time of day."

"You've always been a morning person," I say.

"Yes, and you have never been." She laughs. "You and your father would both sleep till noon if you could."

This is true. Our favorite day of the week is Saturday when we can sleep until nine or ten, eat pancakes, lay around a little longer, then get dressed. Slow and quiet is the way my brain wants to start the day.

"Do you like living here?" Mama asks.

"Yeah, it's all right."

"Have you made friends?" She rubs the back of my hand.

"Haven't been here that long, but I do have one friend — Samantha."

"I'd love to meet her. Why don't you invite her over?"

I let my foot slide along the porch as we glide back and forth. "She doesn't have a telephone. She just kind of shows up." I don't mention the fact that it's been weeks since she has shown up and I'll be sneaking over to her house soon to have another talk with the drunk mama.

"Do you know where she lives? When Frank gets home with the truck, we could ride over and invite her to dinner. Her parents could come too."

The thought of Mama at Sam's or the drunk mama here makes my head spin. It's way too early for my brain to come up with believable lies so I just stare at my feet.

"It's all right if you don't want me to meet them."

I glance up and catch a look on Mama's face that I've seen before. It's the same one I saw when a neighbor lady avoided talking to her after she took a bottle of pills. She turns her head toward the crab apple tree at the side of the porch. "It really is beautiful here."

I take another sip of coffee and hope Daddy doesn't come home from work early. "Mama, of course I want you to meet Sam. In fact, why don't I ride my bike and invite her over?"

"That's a great idea. I'll cook something special for dinner. We'll surprise your Daddy with a little dinner party." She gets up and heads for the door. "What about her parents, will you invite them?"

"Her daddy is," I pause wishing my brain would work, "out of town, and her mama, well, she stays busy."

"All right, then, it will be a dinner for four." She smiles and closes the door.

Is not telling the same as lying? What about lying to keep people from getting hurt? A vision of Brother Jim floats in my head. He bangs his hand down on the pulpit and yells, "A lie is a lie! Good folks don't ever tell lies - not little white ones or big, huge ones."

I look up into the sky as I pedal past Thompson Creek. "Lord, I'm hopin' you're a bit more understanding than Brother Jim. I am trying to do better. It's just, well, sometimes the truth ain't worth telling." As usual, God doesn't answer, which, come to think of it, shows his intelligence. If he ever did yell an answer down, I'd fall out with a heart attack, or maybe even go blind like Paul on the Damascus Road. His plan of answering questions after we get to heaven is much better. Until then, there's always preachers shouting answers whether I want to hear 'em or not.

I speed up when Birch Road comes in view. Oak trees line both sides of the street leading into town. Their huge limbs reach across, and meet in the middle creating a giant umbrella for passengers beneath. This probably saves many a traveler from heat stroke since the four seasons of Pearl are hot, hotter, hottest and Christmas. It's not uncommon to see folks in shorts on Jesus' birthday singing carols about snowmen and sleigh rides. That, along with all the paper snowflakes dangling from tree branches and stuck on windows is why children get so confused on those aptitude tests. Takes some children till third grade to match 30 degrees Fahrenheit with the Christmas tree picture instead of 70 degrees.

I suppose what Pearl lacks in seasons is made up in beauty. 'One of the prettiest places in the South' is the claim made by folks from here, but I say a person needs more than pretty to survive. My dream city has lots of people, an ocean to put my feet in and a huge library. Any place, really, that has a population above nine hundred.

Unfortunately, Daddy doesn't share my dream of big city life. He needs plenty of space. We've moved four times in the past seven years and each move brings more space. No telling where he'll move us next, probably in the middle of the woods somewhere. It can't be further than an hour from the state mental hospital though.

The trip to Sam's takes forty-five minutes. As I park my bike, sweat runs from my body and creates a small lake in the dirt. It must be at least a hundred today.

"Maggie, what you doing here?" Sam motions to follow her round back where I'm overjoyed to find a spot of shade. Sitting next to Sam, my joy quickly turns to anger. Her arms, speckled with yellow and green bruises, poke through a sleeveless shirt and a small cut, almost healed, curves along her jaw.

"Why didn't you come to my house?" I ask.

She shrugs.

"Sam, you promised if she tried to hit you again, you'd come to my house."

"Sometimes, she's too fast for me. Maybe I need to join the track team at school." She pulls a blue marble from her pocket and says, "Got a new one."

I ignore her newest treasure. "Sam, why don't you report her to the sheriff? I'll go with you."

"A couple of years ago I told a teacher what she does. Ya know what happened? Absolutely nothing."

"The sheriff will have to do something."

"Like what? Put me in a foster house? No thanks, at least with mama I know what I get."

"Let me tell Daddy then. He won't let them put you in a foster house."

Sam stands and walks in a circle around me, sending a small cloud of dust in the air. "What's he suppose to do? No Maggie, you can't tell. You promised."

"Samantha Williams, you are one of the most stubborn people I know. Nobody should be used as a punching bag!"

"Come here, I want to show you something," she says.

We walk to the edge of the yard, behind a small shed. Sam leans over, pushes some stones aside, and uncovers a hole in the ground. She pulls out an old shoebox and sits down. With the lid on the ground and the box in her lap she digs through marbles, matchsticks from our poker games, and a birthday card to find a stack of photographs. She pushes them into my hand.

"This is Mama before she drank."

There are four pictures. One of a woman, pants rolled up, standing at the edge of the ocean. Another shows her in a flower garden by a statue of a winged angel. Arms draped around the stone figure, head back with the look of sheer delight on her face. In the last two she's in a wooden rocker, a small girl with copper curls on her lap. They are staring at one another, smiling.

"She didn't always hit me," Sam whispers.

A car horn blows in the distance. I lean back against the shed and close my eyes. I feel Sam beside me; her breaths are long and deep. I slow my breathing to match hers and listen for another horn. How does one become a monster? Is it the same way you go crazy? Maybe everyone has a breaking point where you dive head first into some terrible place never to find your way out. I lay my hand on top of Sam's and whisper, "A doctor once said that Mama's sickness runs in families."

"Won't happen to you," she says.

"How can you know that for sure?"

She squeezes my hand. "The same way I know I'll never be a drunk."

I look at Sam and smile. "I won't say anything to Daddy, but you're coming home with me. Go inside and grab your stuff."

"Can't go in the house, Mama has company."

"You can wear my clothes." I stand ready to hear fifteen reasons why leaving the yard isn't possible.

"She's gonna be mad as a hornet when she can't find me."

"Tack a note to the door."

"No," Sam laughs, "I kind of like the idea of her not knowing."

As we pedal onto Main Street, I pray God will strike the drunk mama dumb and make her forget she has a daughter. ⌒

~ SIXTEEN ~

WHEN SAM FIRST arrived, Mama and Daddy asked about the bruises, but seemed to accept the story of a bike accident, and after five days, they haven't mentioned Sam going home. In fact, it seems everyone would be quite content to keep things just the way they are. Mama has taken to Sam as if she gave birth to her, and Sam can't stop smiling. Daddy laughs more and I'm beginning to believe God has answered my prayer because there hasn't been a single word from the drunk mama. The thought of her roaming through town with no memory at all makes me want to dance around the house like a fool.

"Girls, come here a minute."

Sam brushes against me as she charges out of my room. I follow and make it to Mama's room as she plops down on the bed.

"What do you think?"

"Turn around Miss Elizabeth, so we can see the whole thing."

Mama turns in a small circle. The dress, a shade lighter than her eyes, is cinched at the waist with a black belt. The full bottom falls right below her knees. "Well?"

Sam leans over and smoothes out the bottom of the dress. "You look like one of those fashion models in the magazines at the library."

"I wasn't sure about the color of the dress. There was a red one, but blue is Frank's favorite color."

"You look beautiful, Mama."

She wraps her arm around my shoulder. "I've got an idea. Let's all dress up and have a party. Maggie, put on one of your pretty church dresses and find something nice for Samantha. I'll fix the food while y'all get dressed."

Before we can answer, she's in the hall heading for the kitchen. "Looks like we have to dress up," I moan.

Sam grabs my arm and pulls me toward the door. "It'll be fun."

"What has gotten into you?"

"Me? Aren't you the one who said how wonderful it would be to dress up and go to a fancy party? Well, this can be a practice run."

"Yeah, sure," I say, pretending to be miserable.

"Come on, Maggie, it'll make your mama happy. Besides, it won't kill us to wear dresses and brush our hair. Think how surprised Mr. Frank's gonna be." Sam, still holding my arm, drags me down the hall to my bedroom. A smile slides across my face. "You know we'll have fun."

"Seeing you in a dress will be the most entertaining thing I've experienced since living in Pearl." I open the closet and reach for the fanciest dress hanging. "Here, try this one."

Sam takes the dress and holds it under her chin. Sunlight from the window dances across the blue satin material causing the dress to shimmer and come alive. She whispers, "It's beautiful."

"Try it on."

She slips the dress over her head and I tie the sash. White lace around the collar and belt has kept the thing from coming out of the closet. Mama loves lace, but on me, it looks out of place. Samantha, however, looks like she was born to wear frilly dresses.

"You look pretty," I say, which isn't a lie. "The color matches your eyes. In fact, you can have it."

"You sure, Maggie?"

I nod. "Looks horrible on me."

She runs her hand along the bottom of the dress and smiles. "What about you? What are you gonna wear?"

There is no green dress to match my eyes, so I settle for a brown and white plaid to match with, well nothing really. I slip it on, look in the mirror and wonder how I can be kin to such a beautiful mama.

"That looks nice." Sam smiles and grabs the brush off the dresser. "Come here and let me fix your hair."

"You don't even brush your own hair and suddenly you're a beautician?" I'm sure it's a joke, until I see the hurt look on Sam's face.

"Yeah, you're right," she mumbles.

"Hey, I'm kidding."

"Here," she says sticking the brush toward me. "I don't know how to fix hair."

"Samantha, I'm sorry. Please try to do something with this hair. I gave up on it a long time ago."

She stares for a moment, then smiles. "Do you have any hair ribbon?"

I open the top dresser drawer where barrettes, ribbon and other such items Mama bought are kept. Sam digs around and pulls out bobby pins and a blue ribbon. She motions for me to sit on the bed where, for the next fifteen minutes, I stay while Sam brushes, pulls and ties my hair over and over. Finally, either she stops from exhaustion, or I'm beautiful.

"There, you look better without all that hair in your eyes."

"You sound like Daddy."

"It's true, take a look."

Somehow, Sam has made my straight, plain brown hair look, if not pretty, better than before. I do look better with my bangs pinned back. Daddy will be thrilled to see my eyes.

"Thanks, you did good. Now, it's my turn."

We meet Daddy at the front door. Clothes, dirtier than usual, are covered with insulation; shoulders droop forward as he smiles. "Am I at the wrong house?" He leans over, kisses the top of my head and runs his hand through Sam's curls bound together with a ribbon.

"Mama's putting on a party."

He bends over and unlaces his boots. Pink specks poke through his hair. "Have I missed someone's birthday?"

Mama walks in the living room. "Just celebrating life," she says.

Daddy slips both boots off, then walks over to Mama. He kisses her soft on the lips. "Elizabeth, you look beautiful."

She reaches up and wraps her arms around his neck. "Thank you, now, go get cleaned up so we can get this party started. Will you wear your suit?"

"My suit?" he asks.

"Please." Mama kisses him again.

He smiles and walks to the back of the house. Most men might complain about dressing up on a weeknight, but not Daddy. In fact, if she told him to shave his head and wear his boxers, he would do it with a smile.

Mama switches on the radio and disappears into the kitchen. Sam and I stand by the front door staring at one another while Elvis Presley sings about his good luck charm.

"Should we go help?" Sam asks, pulling on the bottom of her dress. A curl has worked itself loose from the ribbon and dangles by her right ear.

I shrug and move towards the couch. "She'll let us know."

"Oh." Sam joins me on the sofa. "Guess we'll wait here then."

Before we're settled good, Daddy walks in looking about as comfortable as a deer caught in the middle of town.

"You look nice," I say.

Drops of water dive from his head and land on of his brown Christmas suit. He pulls on the skinny gold tie clamped around his neck. "Thanks."

"Yeah, Mr. Frank, you look nice."

He gives Sam a wink. "You don't look half bad yourself."

Mama waltzes in and grabs Daddy's hand. "Food's ready."

Moments later we are gawking at a plate of cheese and crackers, a tray of carrots, celery and pickles, a bowl of little meatballs, and glasses of ice cream punch. I look around for the little party sandwiches.

"Frank, will you say the blessing?"

"Lord, bless this food. Amen." Daddy's always fast when it comes to praying over food; guess he doesn't want it to get cold. Tonight, he could pray for hours because most of the food on the table started out cold.

"This is what rich people eat at parties," Mama explains as she heaps food on the blue china plates.

Never would have dreamed rich folks consider cheese and crackers a meal. Ice cream in the drink ain't a bad idea, but people need more than celery and carrots to survive. It's a miracle they don't all starve to death. I glance at Sam who is busy chomping on a pickle.

"There's chocolate cake after the dance," Mama says.

"What dance?" Daddy mumbles, with three little meatballs stuffed in his mouth.

"It'll be fun." Mama reaches over and squeezes Daddy's hand. "Please, Frank. We haven't danced since Marla's wedding. How long has that been?"

"Around ten years," Daddy says.

"Really, it's been that long? Well, a husband should dance with his wife at least every ten years."

"Yeah, I suppose that's not too much to ask." Daddy stands. "Isn't that your favorite song?"

"Connie Stevens — you remember."

"Can I have this dance?" Daddy gently pulls Mama to her feet and leads her to the living room. Sam and I nearly knock our chairs over trying to get up from the table. We make our way to the couch, while Daddy moves and sways to the music like there isn't a thing on earth he'd rather do right now. Mama lays her head on his shoulder, closes her eyes and lets him guide her around the room.

Next, a man's voice wails about how he can't stop loving someone. Mama nods our way and before I can object, Daddy grabs my hand and spins me around the room. I hear Mama ask Sam to dance.

"Oh, no ma'am, I don't know how."

"It's easy, just follow my lead."

Song after song, the four of us dance around like we're on American Bandstand. The room fills with laughter, and for a moment, I allow myself to believe this will last forever. I imagine this until a knock at the door ends the dance. Racing over, I open the door to find the drunk mama. From the smell, she must have poured whiskey all over herself. I wonder what Daddy would do if I slammed the door in her face. Before I can find out Mama comes between me and her.

"I'm here to get my girl."

"Hello, I'm Elizabeth Wall. You must be Samantha's mother. Please come in. We were just about to have some cake, would you like some?"

"No, just need to get my daughter."

Mama smiles and says, "Thank you for letting Samantha spend time here. She is such a good friend to Maggie."

I don't smile. I'm not nice like Mama.

"This is my husband, Frank."

Daddy walks over and sticks out his hand. The drunk mama shakes it mumbling, "I'm Colleen."

"Nice to meet you, Colleen," Daddy says.

"Won't you join us for some cake and coffee?" Mama asks.

"No, no thanks. My friend's in the car."

Daddy looks toward the couch. "Your friend could join us."

Sam walks over and stands next to her mama. "We need to get home, don't we mama?"

The drunk mama pokes Sam in the belly. "Yeah, tell the people thank you, girl."

"Let me get some cake for you to take home." Mama walks out the room before anyone can say no. A few minutes later, she's back with half a cake wrapped in foil. She places it in Sam's hands.

"Thanks, Miss Elizabeth." Sam holds the cake in one hand and guides the drunk mama off the porch with the other.

"Why couldn't she stay?" I ask.

Mama closes the door. "Samantha's mother wanted her to go home."

"She's not a good mama," I mumble.

Daddy strokes my hair. "Maggie, she's still her mother."

"Well, it ain't right. Sam should live with us, not with that…"

Mama grabs my hand. "Would you like some cake?"

"No thanks, I'm tired. Think I'll go on to bed."

Mama follows me and watches as I climb under the covers. "Are you going to sleep in your dress?"

"Yep," I answer.

She eases down beside me. "Do you want to say prayers?"

"You say 'em tonight."

She takes my hand and closes her eyes. "Lord, thank you so much for today. Help us have a restful night. Please be with Samantha and keep her safe. Also, be with Colleen. Help with her life, Lord. Amen."

"I love you Mama."

She leans over, a mixture of honeysuckle and chocolate, spills over on my face and pillow. "Love you too, Mags," she whispers.

When the door closes, I slip to the floor. The wood planks beneath my knees feel rough and hard. Shifting the weight back on my heels, I close my eyes.

"Lord," I whisper, "I know you're thinking, oh great here's that Maggie girl wasting my holy time again. I admit, sometimes I do ask for silly stuff, like the other day when I prayed my breasts would grow. It seemed like such an important thing to ask for, but now, I realize that was something I should have just kept to myself. I am sorry about that, because I know you stay busy dealing with things down here and running heaven and all. Anyway, I'll try to keep that in mind from now own."

I lean forward determined to stay on my knees.

"Tonight though, Lord, I have some serious praying to do. Now, I'm not going to ask you to slap the drunk mama silly, even though that's not a bad idea, no, I'm gonna be lovin' like Brother Jim yelled about being all the time. So in the spirit of love, send someone to help the drunk mama find her way. And please Lord, keep Sam safe. If you can, figure out a way so she can live with us. She'll make a great sister. Amen. Oh yeah, thank you that Mama is well. Please, keep her that way." ❧

⌐ SEVENTEEN ⌐

"MAGGIE."

"Huh?" Rolling over, I try, without success to open my eyes. My brain is still sleeping and won't send the message, which happens when I shouldn't be awake.

"Maggie."

I rock my head back and forth on the pillow. "What?"

"Meet me in the tree house."

"Tree house?" I mumble. "What time is it?"

"Around five, I think."

"In the morning?" My eyes open slowly as I pull the pillow over my head.

"Come on, Maggie, this is important, huge in fact."

I creep out of bed and stumble to the window. Sam peers in with a smile that should be saved for Christmas morning when you've gotten everything on your list. I close the window and feel my way back to bed.

"Maggie!" The pane vibrates as she bangs the glass.

"All right!" I am back at the window, this time wide-awake.

"What on earth can't wait until, I don't know, daylight?" I open the window and stick one leg through.

"What are you doing?" Sam asks.

"Going to the tree house." When both legs are through the window, I ease myself from the ledge to the ground, careful not to bang my head on the way out. It has been two days since the drunk mama drug Sam away from Mama's party. I lean in closer to get a good look at her arms and face; no new bruises. "This better be good," I moan.

"It's better than good, come on."

Sam leads the way, a flashlight in one hand and a paper sack in the other. I walk close to the stream of light and look out for tree roots, branches, or nocturnal animals creeping about in the dark. As we climb up the ladder, an owl calls out in the distance reminding me I should be in bed.

"I've got something that's going to change our lives." Sam draws the sack close to her chest.

"There in the bag?"

"Yep, this is the answer to all our problems." The Christmas smile is on her face again.

The bag's too small for a shotgun or the cash register from Murray's, neither of which I could deal with right now. It's too big to hold a cigar or cigarettes, besides, even Sam can't claim smoking will change anything.

"So, what do you have?"

"Maggie, my friend, inside this bag is a way to grow breasts."

I stare at Sam, waiting for her to laugh. "You're kidding, right?"

"Would I joke about a subject as serious as this? I was up most of the night figuring it out."

"What on earth are you talking about? Did you find some magic seeds?"

"Don't be ridiculous. No, this is very scientific."

"What then?"

Sam slowly opens the bag and places two boxes on the floor.

"Moon pies? Your answer to growing breasts is moon pies? You got me out of bed for this?"

"Hear me out. You and I, like most of the girls in our class, barely have anything at all while Johnnie Sue's breasts are huge. There has to be a reason. I asked myself what does she do that we don't? I thought about this for a long time, but couldn't come up with anything, so then I asked what does she eat that we don't? That's when I realized Johnnie Sue eats a moon pie every day at lunch. She's been eating them since third grade."

I look at Sam unable to speak. The drunk mama has hit her in the head one too many times. "This is the stupidest thing I've ever heard." As soon as the words are out, I know fists are not the only things that cause pain.

"You're right," she mumbles. "How can I be so stupid?"

"You're not stupid, the idea seems a little, well..."

"Stupid, I know." She wipes her eyes with the back of her hand. "Sorry, I bothered you."

"Maybe God does care about breasts," I say.

"What?"

"I mean, what if you're right? She does eat a lot of moon pies."

"You're just saying that." Sam stuffs the boxes back in the sack.

"No really, it makes sense, kind of."

"You think so, Maggie?" The hope in her voice makes me want to eat the moon pies, box and all.

"The only way we'll find out is by doing an experiment."

"An experiment?" she asks.

"Yeah, we've got to eat us some moon pies."

Sam slips the boxes from the bag. "We can start with these."

"Where did they come from?" I ask.

"Don't worry, I didn't steal them."

"Good, I'd hate for you to go to jail over moon pies. How many do we have to eat?"

"More than this. Do you have any?"

"I think we have some chocolate ones."

"No, they have to be banana. That's the only ones Johnnie Sue eats. Here, we'll each take a box. Do you think you can buy some more?"

"How many more are we going to need?"

"A bunch." Sam rips open the box and pulls out a round, yellow miracle worker. "Go on, we need to start eating 'em."

"A glass of milk would be nice," I say and take a bite.

Streaks of yellow light flood my room as I crawl back in bed with an empty box and a stomach that may burst wide open any moment. I want breasts as much as the next girl, but there has to be an easier way to grow them. One more banana moon pie might just kill me.

"Lord, I wasn't going to waste your time with stuff like this, but if you can just anoint these little cakes. I mean you did turn water into wine and raise people from the dead, so this is really a small job. Anyway, it would mean so much to Sam for this crazy idea of hers to work. Thanks."

I don't expect God to answer all my prayers. I mean, he's not some genie waiting to grant my every wish, however, answers to the important ones would be nice. Maybe, it just takes awhile for prayers to make their way to heaven, or perhaps he doesn't listen to liars. If that's the case, Sam and I will be eating moon pies for a very long time.

"Maggie, are you awake?"

I roll over to see Mama standing by the bed. "Uh-huh."

"I'm going to town."

"How you getting there?" I sit up slowly and rub my expanded belly.

"Your daddy left me the truck. He rode to work with Milton. I'm working on a surprise for y'all."

"Yeah, what kind?" I ask.

She grins and answers, "Can't tell you."

I sit up, throw my legs over the side of the bed and grab her hand. "I want to go."

"That will ruin the surprise. I won't be gone long. Do you want breakfast before I leave?"

I shake my head. "Could you pick up some banana moon pies?" I say, barely able to get out the words.

"Sure. By the way, where does Samantha live?"

"Cross the tracks at Sixth and Main, why?"

"I'm just wondering."

Looking at her black skirt, white blouse, and heels, I can't imagine her anywhere near the drunk mama's house. "Daddy doesn't want us over there, says it's not safe." I look at the floor.

"I'll remember that the next time you ask to go." She walks back to the bed and kisses the top of my head. "Love you, Mags."

"Love you too," I mumble. A trip to Sam's just got harder. ↩

∽(EIGHTEEN)∼

WITH MAMA GONE surprise shopping and Sam doing Lord only knows what, I make my way to the Clarks'. Don't know when it happened, but life just doesn't seem right without a visit with Bea. At first my trips were driven by a need for cookies, but now I'd go even if her oven broke.

"Morning Maggie, come on in. I've got myself a situation back in the kitchen."

"What's wrong? You need some help?" I follow Bea past Miss Clark's office.

She moves quickly down the hall and goes straight to the refrigerator. "No child, there's not a thing you can do. I've been caught with my pants down is all."

I stare at Bea's blue flowered housedress. "Did Mr. Anthony see?"

Her head is in the freezer as she digs through packs of meat. She pulls out something wrapped in white paper and places it on the counter. "See what?"

"You know," I pause, not wanting to say more.

Bea looks my way and for a moment doesn't speak. Then, a smile takes over her face and erupts into laughter. For a solid minute, she laughs, arms and belly jiggling, tears running down her dark face. Finally, she stops long enough to say, "My word, nobody but my mama has seen that!" After a few knee slaps and more tears, the fit ends. "Oh Maggie girl, just means I'm not prepared."

My face burns as I look at the floor and mumble, "Oh."

"I wasn't laughing at you, well, maybe just a little." She grins. "Look at it this way; you just made my day a whole lot better."

"Glad to be of help."

"Now don't be mad." She moves to the sink and turns on the hot water. "In this life, you gotta learn to laugh at yourself. Can't be too serious about things."

I lift myself onto the counter next to the sink. "So, what's the big situation?"

"Wasn't suppose to be a need for dinner tonight because they were going out of town. Been planning the trip for weeks. Then, Miss Clark goes and changes her mind. She just called and said she wants roast for dinner. Roast! Don't matter that it's frozen solid or that there's not a carrot in the house. No, she can't be bothered with little details like that."

"Just tell her you can't cook it. Tell 'em to stop by the diner for supper."

Bea shakes her head. "Yeah, and sure as a dog will bark at the moon, I'll be looking for a new job."

I shake my head. One conversation without the need for a translator would be nice. "She wouldn't fire you over a frozen roast."

Bea plops the meat in the water. "She's done it three times. The last time, I even packed my bags. Only stayed because of Mr. Anthony. He was so pitiful, begging me and all, plus I didn't have any place to go."

"If she throws a fit, come to my house. Mama would love the company." I reach over, open the rooster jar and remove an oatmeal cookie, raisins poking out on both sides.

"She's just high strung is all, poor woman."

"Bea, the lady has more money than the president."

"Money don't make you rich, Maggie. Miss Clark's as empty as that cookie jars gonna be in about fifteen minutes." She smiles and hands me another one. "Stuff can't fill the empty spots. No, ever since she lost her baby, she's been angry at the whole world."

"How did she lose her baby?" I ask.

"Died at four days old. A little boy, pretty as can be. Doctor said just one of those things that happens. Maggie, everyone has a cross to bear. You just got to decide what to do with it. Some folks get weighed down and stop living, others get stronger." Bea pours two glasses of milk and grabs herself a cookie.

I stare out the kitchen window, past the clothesline, to an oak tree heavy with Spanish moss. A picture of Samantha carrying the drunk mama comes to mind. "What if the cross you got to bear ain't worth toting around?"

"Don't know if we get to decide that."

"We should have a say about those things. What if our cross is mean as a snake?"

"You talking about Samantha?"

I nod and take a bite of cookie. "That mama of hers is no good."

Bea closes her eyes for a few seconds. "Maggie, the good Lord loves all his children."

"Well, Sam's one of his children. How come he gave her such a no good mama?"

"I don't know why some things are the way they are, but I do know God's always there to give his peace and strength. Some folks don't seem to want it, though. They spend all their lives running away from him, trying to do things their own way. From what I can tell, that's just a waste of time."

"You sound like Mama."

Bea smiles and ask, "How's she doing?"

"Good."

"You know she came and saw me the other day. Brought me a bunch of flowers. No one ever done that before." She walks into the pantry and comes out with a sack of onions. "Said she wanted to thank me for being such a good neighbor. Your mama is one fine lady."

I swirl the last of the milk around the bottom of the glass. "You never told anybody about the day we came over looking for a telegraph machine, did you?"

"Far as I'm concerned it never happened. Just glad she's better."

"Yeah, me too," I say. "This time I think she's well for good. Sometimes, I reckon, a person's cross can be taken from them."

Bea rubs my hand. "Yeah, I suppose."

When I get home, lights are on, but no sign of Mama. A box of moon pies, opened with one missing, proves she's been here. I grab one, gulp it down in three bites, and peek down my blouse. Everything is just as it was before Sam's scheme, flat as the kitchen floor. I reach for another pie, but the sound of laughter saves me from eating the thing.

"Mama, that you?" I call out.

A voice floats in through the kitchen window. "Maggie, we're in the back, but don't come out. You'll ruin the surprise."

"Sam?"

"Yeah, I'm helping."

Mama walks through the backdoor, a shovel in one hand, and a straw hat in the other. "Maggie, you've got to stay inside until your daddy gets home. We'll be finished by then."

"What on earth are you doing?"

"You'll see. Just don't look out the window." Grinning, she walks back outside.

I pick the California travel book up from the coffee table and plop down on the couch. This sure is turning out to be a strange day. I flip through the book, then read a few chapters in *The Lost Horizon*. Finally, the doorknob moves.

"You're home!"

Daddy walks in, brown paper bag in hand. "Hey, Mags, glad to see you too. Where's my truck?"

"Out back, guess its part of the big surprise. I've had to stay inside all afternoon while Mama and Sam get ready. Do you have any idea what they're up to?"

"No, here, put these on the counter. Milton sent more tomatoes."

I take the bag and walk into the kitchen. "Well, I think Mama may be digging a swimming hole out there. She came in once with a shovel, and not fifteen minutes ago walked outside wearing a bathing suit."

"You don't say." Daddy opens the refrigerator, stares inside, then closes the door empty handed.

"Mama," I yell, "Daddy's home. Can we come out?"

At first there's no answer, then Sam calls out, "Not yet."

I move toward the door. "I can't wait another second."

"Hang on, Maggie." Daddy catches my hand and pulls me towards the couch. "You don't want to spoil your Mama's fun. It won't be much longer."

"Oh, all right." I sink next to him on the sofa. "How was work?"

"Mr. Tarver asked me to run a job, you know, be the foreman."

I look at him close to make sure it's not a joke. He smiles, all proud. "Daddy, that's great! You could run that whole company. Will you get a raise? Even if you don't, the fact that you'll be the boss is something."

"Well, yeah, if I take it."

"Why wouldn't you? Don't you want to be in charge?"

"The job's in Carlson which means I'd be getting home later and have to work half days on Saturday." He leans over and brushes wood shavings from his sock. "Your Mama's doing good now, but, well, a foreman can't miss a lot of work. It's a big responsibility."

The good feelings from Mama's surprise day begin to float toward the ceiling. I close my eyes. "She's doing so good, Daddy. I think those electrical treatments were a cure. You know things like that happen sometimes."

He brushes bangs from my eyes. "I've got the weekend to make a decision. Don't mention it to your Mama, hear?"

I'm about to say a choice to be boss should take two minutes, not two days, when Sam walks through the back door. Eyes, barely seen, peer out from under a straw hat big enough to provide shade for a family of four. "Y'all can come out now."

Daddy grins. "Hope there's food out there because I'm half starved to death."

"Wait 'til you see, Mr. Frank." Sam catches the hat as it slides down her face. "Come on, Maggie."

I follow behind as Sam rambles on about how we're not going to believe what all they've done. What I can't believe is Sam walking around with a hat the size of Texas on her head. Just three weeks around Mama has turned the girl inside out. I do believe if Mama told her to paint herself green and hop around on one foot, she'd do it and smile.

Samantha tears out the door while I stand on the steps with my mouth open. The yard is now sand and a blue pool overflowing with water. Where white blends into grass, a red umbrella shades two beach chairs. Daddy crosses the sand and pulls Mama into his arms.

She tilts the straw hat away from her face and smiles. "Don't worry, a feast awaits you over on the picnic table."

"I can't believe you pulled this off," Daddy says.

"What do you think of the bridge? Samantha painted it all by herself." Mama points toward a plywood Golden Gate Bridge leaning against a pine tree. "Maggie, we can't get you to San Francisco, so we brought it here."

I'm no expert, only seen beaches in books, but even people from California would admit Mama's beach looks good. I want to say this is the best surprise of my life, better than anything she could have done, but all that comes out is, "I love everything."

Mama hands us each a glass of punch from the table. "Before you girls take a dip, let's have a toast." She lifts her glass and says, "To our beach vacation."

People say nothing in life is perfect, but today is pretty close to just that. The wade pool is our Pacific Ocean, the sand our island. Sam and I come out of the water long enough to build sand castles and eat pieces of fruit on toothpicks, while Daddy and Mama lounge under the umbrella. Every now and then, I close my eyes and listen to them laugh, wanting this day to last forever. By dark, our fingers look like they belong to old women and our backs burn from the sun. Even so, we argue when Mama insists we go inside.

"Please, Mama, just a little longer," I beg.

She waves her hand through the air. "Maggie, the mosquitoes are going to carry us off."

Daddy picks up the towels and walks over to the pool. "The beach will be here tomorrow."

"Oh, all right," I moan.

With towels wrapped around our waist we walk inside, leaving Mama's beach and our perfect lives behind. ‿

~ NINETEEN ~

TODAY WILL MARK a new record - a whole week since a lie has escaped my lips. Now I know how Babe Ruth felt when he set that baseball record. Seven days probably wouldn't seem like much to ole Babe, but to me, it's huge. Feels good to be back with the upstanding, truth telling, citizens of America. Maybe I won't burn in hell after all.

"What ya doing?" Mama walks in the kitchen, spit curls all over her head.

"Nothing," I mumble, mouth full of banana moon pie.

She sits next to me at the table. "You sure do love those things. Never seen anyone eat so many." I push an unopened pie in her direction, careful not to even nod my head in agreement. She shoves it back. "No thanks, one a week is about all I can stand."

"Why's your hair all pinned up?" I ask eager to change the subject.

"I'm trying something new. When the pins come out, my head should be covered with soft, beautiful, curls. That's what I'm hoping for anyway." She takes a sip from my glass of milk. "Maggie, have you heard from Samantha this week?"

"No, ma'am, why?"

"Just wondering why we haven't seen her since the beach vacation."

I lift the glass and gulp down the milk. This is more dangerous ground than the moon pies. Conversations about Sam usually include about a hundred lies. I shrug my shoulders and pray a curl will spring loose.

"Y'all aren't mad at one another are you?"

"No ma'am, we're still friends." I smile. "Think I'll go ride my bike. Good luck with your hair." I'm out the door before she can ask any more questions. Not telling lies feels a lot like gym class, both are exhausting.

I stop on Thompson Creek long enough to throw a few rocks into the water below, then head to Sam's house; the destination of my bike ride determined the moment Mama mentioned her name. My record's still intact though. I've decided leaving information out is not the same as lying. Brother Jim would probably argue this point, but thankfully, he's not here.

I park the bike by the front porch and walk around back expecting to see Sam behind the shed. The rocks are standing guard over the buried treasure, but she's no where to be found. I open my mouth to yell her name, but quickly yank it shut. Even though it's four in the afternoon, the drunk mama may be sleeping. Sneaking Sam to my house will be easier without her to deal with. I walk around front, hop on the porch and tap lightly on the front door. Nothing, so I knock a little harder. The door creaks opens.

"Sam?" The smell of stale cigarettes and whiskey hit me as I step inside the living room. To the left I see the kitchen. Dirty dishes are on the counter, trash overflows from a small garbage can in the corner, but no Sam. I walk to the only piece of furniture in the room and peer over the top. What I see behind the sofa sends a wave of nausea through my body so strong I nearly fall to the floor. Choking back a scream, I run out the door and down the steps. I race through the yard to the building across the street, not stopping until I'm inside.

"Hey," someone barks from behind the bar. "What are you doing in here?"

I follow the voice through the dim lit room to its owner, an overstuffed bear of a man. "Need to use your phone," I manage to say.

His face crunches into a frown. "I don't need no trouble and you look like you're in a whole mess of it."

"Please, I just need to use the phone." My voice sounds high and strange, like it belongs to someone else.

He grunts and motions to the back wall. "Better be quick."

I move towards the wall, then stop. My throat begins to tighten. "I, I, don't have any money."

The bear leans against the bar, eyes narrow and dark. "Sorry kid, pay phone's all we got. You better get out of here and go home."

This can't be happening! I stumble out the door. Total panic has replaced the nausea. I take out across the parking lot, but stop halfway to the street. Our truck is in front of Sam's house.

"Daddy!" I scream.

His head jerks my way. Before I can move, he's running across the street, confusion and fear etched across his face. "What happened? Maggie, are you all right?"

I fall into his arms and sob.

He pushes me back to look at my face. "What did they do to you?" He's staring at Red's Bar, eyes wild with anger.

"No, Daddy, it's not me. In the house... Sam. . . . I think ... I think she's dead." My eyes close as I fall against him.

He lifts me in his arms and carries me to where Mama is standing by the truck. "Elizabeth, wait here."

I bury my face into Mama's shaking body. She strokes my hair. "Don't worry, Maggie, we're here. Everything will be all right." I look up. Her eyes open wide and the color drains from her face as, "Oh, dear God," falls from her lips.

Everything seems to speed up. Daddy and Mama are in the truck with Sam between them, her head in Mama's lap. I'm in the back, barely aware of the wind pushing against me, as we speed to the hospital. I close my eyes and see Sam's blood covered body.

Before we should be, we're parked in back of County General. Daddy runs, Sam in his arms, through the emergency door while Mama and I climb from the truck. I follow her to the desk at the front of the waiting room.

"My husband just came in with Samantha Williams. Can we go back?"

The nurse glances at Mama and smiles. "You'll need to wait here. Someone will be with you shortly."

"But my husband is back there. I need to be with Samantha." The words, meant to be strong, sound more like a plea.

"Tell you what, honey, I'll go back and check." With the smile still plastered on her face, she disappears behind the double metal doors.

"We might as well sit down," Mama says, "This may take awhile."

We sit in folding chairs closest to the doors and I stare at the County General Emergency Room plaque leaning against a stack of books on the nurse's desk. Without that sign I wouldn't believe we're in the right place. No sirens announce the arrival of patients, no masked doctors running in and out saving lives; nothing at all what a hospital should be. Even the bright blue walls are wrong.

I sigh and glance back toward the sliding glass door we just ran through. A Coke machine stands on one side, and the oldest, living human in Pearl sits on the other. His head is propped against the wall, eyes shut tight, mouth open wide enough to see tonsils. Snow colored hair, twists in uncontrolled waves toward a prune face. Without the rise and fall of his chest, I'd swear he's been dead for days.

Mama grabs my hand. I look up to see a brave smile on her face. "Did she talk in the truck?" I ask.

"A little," Mama says softly.

I let out a deep sigh, unaware that I had been holding my breath. "What'd she say?"

"She kept saying she had fallen."

I stare at Mama, sure I had misunderstood. "Fell?"

"Yes. I guess that could explain the cut on her head, maybe the eye, but she's in such bad shape. It doesn't make sense." Anger explodes from my brain and drowns out the words. How can she still need to protect the drunk mama? Why would she want to? "Maggie, do you know what could have happened? Did you see anything?"

A burning sensation rises in the back of my throat, and my head pounds. "I didn't see anything," I mumble.

"Remember a few weeks ago when Samantha had all those bruises? What did you say happened?"

I turn my eyes away and rub my forehead. A thousand lies race around my head. Which one had been told? She fell out of the tree house? No, not that time. Was in a car accident? No, never used that one, the drunk mama doesn't have a car. My heart begins to slow. "Bike wreck."

"A bike wreck?" She rolls the words around on her tongue. "Maggie, it's important that we know what happened to Samantha so we can help."

Before I answer, Daddy walks into the waiting room. He sits next to Mama, but keeps his eyes on my face. "Most of the blood came from the gash in her head. It took seven stitches to close it up. By morning she'll have a black eye, and," he clears his throat, "some nasty bruises on her body. Two of her ribs are broken."

"When can she go home?" Mama asks.

"They're not saying. She's pretty bad off. Doctor says it looks like she was kicked in the head." Daddy leans towards me. "Maggie, did you see anyone around the house?"

My hands slip to the edge of the chair. "No sir, didn't see anything."

Mama grips Daddy's arm. "Frank, we need to find Colleen."

Before I can stop myself, I'm on my feet. "Why do you have to find her?"

"Maggie, she's her mother," Mama says.

Daddy studies me for a moment then asks, "Is there some reason we shouldn't look for Colleen?"

"How should I know?"

He moves beside me. "Elizabeth, you two go home. I'll stay here."

Mama opens her mouth to speak, but, instead, nods in agreement. We walk past the sleeping man, through the sliding glass doors to the truck. She cranks the engine and drives out of the parking lot without speaking. I stare out the window, fighting back tears.

A friend would be praying right now, asking for God's help — begging for his help, in fact, but I can't seem to get out one single prayer. I'm too busy thinking up ways to kill the drunk mama. By the time we get home, I've gone through three different scenarios - one involving a gun, another a rope, and the last a baseball bat. My favorite is the bat.

"Maggie, are you going to come inside?"

"Yeah," I mumble.

We walk in and Mama collapses on the sofa. I walk to the window and stare at my hands wondering if they can kill.

"Maggie, what's going on?"

My stomach tightens. "What do you mean?" I look out at San Francisco. One of the chairs has fallen over, but everything else - the beach, the pool, the bridge, - remains perfect.

Mama sighs. "Mags, you need to tell me if you know anything that will help Samantha."

"It's, well, it's. . ." I stuff my hands in the pocket of my jeans to stop the shaking.

"Do you have any idea where we can find Colleen?"

I shake my head. "Ask Mr. Anthony."

"Why would Mr. Anthony know?"

"Just ask him, Mama," I mumble and walk out the room. After locking the door, I climb in bed. I try to sleep, but one thought keeps playing over in my mind: if she dies, it's my fault. ⌁

~(TWENTY)~

THE NEXT MORNING Mama wakes me with a cup of coffee milk. She sits on the end of the bed, but says nothing. I stare at the blue flower on the saucer, afraid to ask about Sam. I take a few sips and wait. When the cup is almost empty, she stands and walks to the door.

"Maggie, we're going to the hospital."

"Will you let me know how she's doing?"

"You can come with us." When I don't respond, she says, "We'll probably be late. Are you sure you don't want to come?"

The look on her face brings tears to my eyes. I want to admit that I'm a liar and this is all my fault. I need to tell her all about the drunk mama, but instead I just look away. "No ma'am, maybe tomorrow."

When they leave, I throw on clothes and run to the Clarks'. I find Bea on the back porch, coffee cup in one hand, Bible in the other.

"Maggie, any news on Samantha?"

I shake my head. "How did you hear?"

"Your mama came over last night. When she left, Mr. Anthony took out of here like the house was on fire. He stayed out all night looking for Colleen."

"Did he find her?"

"Not yet. He came home, changed clothes and left again. He's the only one, this side of eternity who can talk sense into that woman."

"Will he go see Sam?"

Bea moves to the door. "Already has. Come on and I'll fix you some breakfast."

She walks to the kitchen, moving slower than usual, and motions towards the table. "How 'bout fried eggs and grits?" She pulls out the black iron skillet, and disappears in the pantry.

"What did Miss Clark say about all this?"

Bea appears with a white sack and eggs and doesn't answer until the meal's cooked. "Here, eat it all, you look a little sickly this morning." After pouring a fresh cup of coffee, she joins me at the table. "Miss Clark's in Texas somewhere. Left yesterday to buy equipment for the factory."

"That's probably best." I pick up the fork and move the food from one side of the plate to the other.

"Maggie, I'm gonna get right to it. I know you're upset, but if you can help these folks figure out what happened to Samantha, you need to do it quick. Someone from the bar told your daddy a black man was seen hanging around outside Samantha's house. Don't know if that's true, but I do know this, if the sheriff gets involved, there won't be a black man in Pearl safe."

"What do you mean?"

"Just believe me when I say you don't want the sheriff getting involved in this." She pauses to take a sip of coffee. "Maggie, it's time for you to tell the truth about Colleen."

"What?"

"Wasn't hard to figure out. Why else would you hate that woman so much? Besides, it's not possible for one girl to be so clumsy."

"Why didn't you tell?"

"Lord forgive me, I should have. Maybe Samantha wouldn't be laid up in the hospital if I had." She pulls a handkerchief out and dabs her eyes.

Looking away, I mumble, "This isn't your fault, it's mine."

"Honey, there's plenty of blame to go around. What's done is done, but we can sure do different from now on."

"But I've told so many lies."

Bea reaches over and pats my hand. "Yes, you have. Can't take 'em back either, but you can tell the truth now. Where are your folks?"

"Hospital," I mumble.

"I'm gonna call and get them over here so y'all can talk."

"No, I'll wait until they get home."

"Maggie, it needs to be done now. You can do this." She eases up from the chair. "Try and eat, child, you're as pale as Miss Clark's linen tablecloth." She walks out of the room mumbling, "It's time for everyone to do what's right by that child."

When Mama arrives, I'm still at the kitchen table staring at my untouched food. I throw a dishtowel over the plate and shove it to the center of the table.

"Maggie, honey, are you all right?" Mama asks, walking into the room. I can't see my face or the tablecloth, but I'd bet all the tea in China, hers is whiter than either one. She sits down beside me, eyes swollen and red. "Bea said you needed to talk."

"Yes ma'am." I move to the sink, turning my back towards her. "Mama, all of this is my fault. I should have done something months ago. Should have told Daddy or Mr. Anthony."

"Mags, honey, what are you talking about?"

"Sam didn't fall; she didn't have bike accidents or fall out the tree house. Her mama gets drunk and beats her. It's all been lies, Mama. I'm nothing but a liar." I lean against the counter and wait to hear her heart break.

"Maggie, I want you to listen to me. You are not responsible for this."

"But if I would have told the truth, maybe someone could have done something to keep this from happening."

"We don't know it was Colleen who did this."

"It was her all right because Sam said she fell. Don't know why she keeps trying to protect that woman."

"Because she loves her," Mama says.

"Well, she shouldn't."

"Maggie, Colleen loves Samantha, too. I'm sure she hates herself for hurting Sam. There's no excuse for what's been done, and it can never happen again, but we have to help both of them."

I spin around to convince her that we don't need to lift one finger to protect the drunk mama. I want to say she's not worth our help and how I wish she'd do everybody a favor and drink herself to death. I open my mouth, but quickly swallow my words and turn back around. I grip the counter and fight back tears. Mama has a way of taking on everyone else's pain, and by the look on her face, this is way too much hurt for one person to carry.

"Maggie, don't worry, things will work out."

Visions of Sam laying in a pool of her own blood floods my mind and I worry my legs won't hold. I move to Mama, sit on the floor and place my head in her lap. "Is she going to die?" I whisper.

Mama lifts my face and kisses my cheek. "Don't even think that, Mags. Samantha's strong, she'll get through this. I need to get back. Will you be all right?"

"Yes ma'am."

"You want to stay here or go home?"

"I'll stay with Bea."

We stand and she gives me a quick hug. When she's gone, I walk back to the window. A red bird lands on the sill, looks at me, then darts over to Bea's flower garden. It hovers above the sea of yellow, red and gold, then flies away. I wish for wings to follow.

People handle worry in different ways. Some stay in bed, others cry, Bea cooks. I've spent the entire day watching her bake. A blackberry cobbler is in the refrigerator next to a batch of ambrosia, three dozen oatmeal cookies are on plates wrapped with foil, and a chocolate cake's in the middle of the table. Hushpuppies wait to be fried after the okra; jambalaya was put on the stove an hour ago, along with a huge pot of spaghetti sauce and meatballs. If we don't get word from the hospital soon, the whole town will have to come over and eat up all this food before Miss Clark gets home. She won't take kindly to Bea's cooking so much, no matter what the reason.

"Mercy, child, it's almost midnight. You must be exhausted."

"I'm fine," I say, rubbing my eyes.

"Maybe I'll make some fudge."

"Bea, what are you going to do with all of this?"

She spoons okra from the skillet and looks at me like I'm talking a foreign language. "People need to eat."

"How many you planning on feeding?" I ask.

"Well, your mama and daddy, Mr. Anthony, you, Colleen if they ever find her, and Samantha will need to eat plenty when she comes home." She shoves a green pitcher my way. "Make yourself useful and add a cup of sugar to the tea."

"Please don't cook anything else. Miss Clark's gonna fire you for sure this time."

She rolls her eyes, but before she can reply the phone rings. I hold my breath as she walks to the black phone hanging on the wall. "Hello. Yes sir, oh praise the Lord. What about Colleen? Good, all right, then good-bye."

I jump from the counter. "What? What did he say? How's Sam?"

Bea wipes her face with a handkerchief. "Samantha's good. The doctor said he'll let her go home tomorrow afternoon. She has to stay in bed, rest for a week or so, but she's coming home."

I fall into the chair and smile for the first time in three days. "Did he say where she's going to stay? I mean she can't go to her house."

"She's coming to yours."

"You mean it? No use even trying to find her mama. Sam can live with us from now own. I need to clean out my closet and chest of drawers to make room for her stuff."

"Hold on, Maggie, you need to take one day at a time. She's staying with y'all until she's healed up. Mr. Anthony didn't say anything about her living with you."

"Well, she has to. Anyway, after this she's not gonna want to be anywhere near that mama of hers."

"You can't know for sure." Grease pops as Bea loads the skillet with hushpuppies. "Lord have mercy, what am I gonna do with all this food?"

"You can always sell plates at church Sunday."

Bea laughs. "Grab a knife and cut into that cake."

"I'm only doing this to help you out. You want a piece?"

She nods. "Pour us some milk, too." ⌐

~⟨ TWENTY-TWO ⟩~

FROM THE AMOUNT of sunlight pouring through the window, I assume the promise of an early morning has been broken. The decision was made last night when Mama tucked me in, but for the life of me, I can't remember why. I fight to clear my brain from too much sleep. Something seems wrong. It's Saturday; along with cries not to sleep my life away, cartoons should be blaring from the television.

I slide from the bed, stumble, eyes closed, to the door and stand in front of Mama's latest addition - a full-length mirror. She attached it without explanation, but I think she hopes it will remind me to brush my hair. I push bangs aside, take a peek and moan. Even a brush can offer no help this morning. Overnight, the freckles have multiplied; my hair, except for the occasional tangle, hangs limply to my shoulders, and my eyes are swollen almost shut. I touch the mirror. "Looks like you've been beaten with a huge stick."

The words slice through the air, cutting the fog from my brain. Sam, the blood, my confession to Mama, all seen clearly now. I grab clothes and head for the bathroom. They'll be here soon.

✺

Sam leans back against the stack of pillows. She touches the gauze bandage wrapped around her head and closes the eye that isn't swollen shut. "How bad do I look?"

"Like something out of a horror movie," I say from across the bedroom.

"That awful, huh?"

"Just kidding, you don't look so bad," I lie.

"Yeah," she mumbles, eye still closed.

I look at the rag doll in my hands and move to the bed. "Got you something."

She doesn't respond. "This here's Gracie Lou. Daddy bought her when I was five. I use to sleep with her." I stop, then confess, "still do, sometimes." I place her on the bed. "Thought she might help."

She lifts the doll with one hand, runs the other along the bottom of Grace Lou's dress, then places it back on the bed. She sucks in air through clenched teeth and stares at the ceiling. I search for something, anything, to make her smile. After a few minutes of searching, I come up with another lie.

"I've got some great news," I begin. "Ya know all those moon pies we've been eating? They're working." She looks toward my flat chest. "Well, you can't tell in my clothes yet, but I swear they're growing. Looks like I've been stung by a wasp now, but come fall they'll be bigger than Johnnie Sue's."

Her grin is worth my lie, even though I promised to stop telling them. "That would be something," she says, then goes quiet again. I watch the smile disappear into a thin, straight line.

"Sam, please don't be mad at me. I had to tell the truth."

She stares at me, but says nothing. Mama's voice keeps me from falling to my knees and begging. "Samantha, you have a visitor. May we come in?"

I don't believe it possible, but Sam's face gets paler, as if the last bit of blood has drained from her body. Her hands move nervously along the quilt, and she opens her mouth but doesn't speak. I move toward the door, ready to turn the lock. "Sam?"

She shifts, sitting straighter, and places Gracie Lou on her lap. "Come in," she says.

I lean against the wall when the door opens, which is the only reason I don't tumble to the floor. There, in the middle of Mama and Daddy, stands Mr. Anthony Clark, starched white shirt, shiny shoes and all. I look around the room, thankful for the earlier decision to stuff dirty underwear in the closet.

Daddy glances my way. "Maggie, we need to talk to Samantha. Will you wait outside, please?"

"She can stay," Sam says.

I take a deep breath, pushing down the urge to sob. Forgiveness comes so easy to Sam. I take a step toward the bed, then lean back against the wall. Probably better to stay out of the way.

Mr. Anthony clears his throat. "Samantha, how are you?"

Sam looks at me and I roll my eyes. "Been better," she says.

Beads of sweat pop out on Mr. Anthony's forehead. "Well, uh, of course." He looks at the floor, then back at Sam. "I want to help."

"Don't need your help," she mumbles.

Mr. Anthony looks back at Mama. She walks over and sits on the bed. "Samantha, Mr. Anthony's being very kind. He's come up with a plan, of sorts, that may work for you and your mother."

"What?"

Mr. Anthony steps closer. "I found your mama this morning. She doesn't remember most of what happened, but she's very sorry for what she did. She's agreed to get help. I brought her to the hospital, so they can help get the alcohol out of her system. When she's better, I'll get her a job at the diner and then you can go back home. We'll keep a close eye on things, of course."

Mama takes Sam's hand. "You only have to go back if that's what you want. You can live here with us."

"Thank you, Miss Elizabeth." She glances at me, then says, "Mr. Anthony, I appreciate the way you're helping Mama."

"Let me know, if there's anything at all that you need."

Sam's eyes close and Daddy shuffles everyone out the room. I promise to leave after a few minuets, so he lets me stay. When they're gone I cross the room and sit on the end of the bed.

"Did you hear that? You can live with us. You don't ever have to leave."

She takes a deep breath. "I'm real thankful for your folks. Never had anyone treat me so good. It's just, well, what about mama?"

"What do you mean?"

"I'm all she's got."

"Please tell me you're not considering going back, not after what she's done. At least stay here awhile. Give her some time, ya know, see how she does."

"Guess so," she mumbles.

"Pinky swear," I say. A pinky swear can be broken, but it's better than a regular, every day promise. A blood promise would be the absolute best, but from Sam's pale face, she needs every drop of blood she's got. "Sam?"

She hesitates, then sticks out her little finger. I wrap my finger around hers and shake.

"You rest. I'll be back later."

She cradles Gracie Lou in her arms. "Thanks, Maggie."

I close the door and look for Mama. She's out back, in a folding chair, staring at the gum ball tree at the edge of the beach. When I sit beside her, she looks at me and smiles.

"She's taking a nap," I say. "Can't believe Mr. Anthony suggested she go back and live with her mama."

Mama glides her finger along the top of the coffee cup she's holding. "Maggie, I'm going to be away from the house some days. I'll need you to help out more, maybe cook dinner a night or two."

"Where you going?"

"I need to spend time with Colleen."

I jump up and wheel around to face her. My hands fly to my hips as if controlled by someone else. "Why on earth would you waste your time with her?"

"Please sit back down."

"No! You don't need to spend your days with that woman. How can you want to help her after what she's done?"

Mama looks past me. "She's still a human being. The folks around here stopped seeing Colleen a long time ago. We can't do that, Maggie."

"Let Mr. Anthony help. Didn't you hear what he said?"

Mama takes a deep breath. I notice, for the first time, the dark shadows under her eyes, and the deep crease between her brow. "We can't pretend Colleen doesn't exist." She stands, takes a few steps and stops. "Maggie, hate is a strange thing, it mostly hurts the one doing the hating."

I dig my toes in the sand and watch Mama disappear through the back door. A warm breeze pushes across the beach bringing with it a distant yelp of a dog. Sounds like a hound lost in the woods. Another round of barks drifts my way, and then fades to nothing. I want to see the world her way, to believe every single person on this earth is worth something, that no matter how much bad is done, they're still worth forgiving. Trouble is, I just don't believe it, and pretending I do makes no sense. ❧

~ TWENTY-THREE ~

M Y NEW LIFE, the one where I have a sister, begins with breakfast and poetry. Mama props up
in bed and fills the air with words from Emily
Dickinson and Robert Frost. She reads of hope and life, of
a road not taken and love never found. Most days for the
last five weeks, have begun this same way. Sam and I usually
can't make sense of the poems, but the way Mama says the
words is nice, so we listen.

After the breakfast dishes are washed and put away, Mama
leaves on the daily trip to town. I tell Sam she's gone to the
library or to Sunshine to pick up groceries. I refuse to say she's
visiting the drunk mama. In fact, I avoid that topic as if the
mention of her name will cause foaming at the mouth and a
slow, painful death. My plan is to keep Sam's thoughts away
from her other home, so she'll stay in mine.

I've wanted a sister all my life. Don't know how many hours
went to dreaming up the perfect one. She was always a year

younger than me, but my size, so we could share clothes. She liked to read, play cards, and catch fireflies just like me. She always laughed at my jokes and thought I was the most intelligent person around. In short, the sister in my dreams was a lot like a mindless robot - smiling and agreeing with everything that came out of my mouth.

Sam is nothing like that sister. She seldom agrees with anything I say, she hates to read, will only play poker, and she'd just as soon as step on a firefly as catch one. But, she listens for hours when I read aloud, will play poker any time of the day or night, and never stomps on the insects I catch. She is in fact, much better than the perfect sister I dreamed about.

Only one person threatens my new life, and so far Sam hasn't mentioned her name, to me anyway. She does get reports from Mama each day. That's when I suddenly have something of great importance to do, like wash my hair. Anything not to hear Mama say how good Colleen's getting along, or how the house is so much better. Mama spent a solid week cleaning the inside, while some colored men, hired by Mr. Anthony, painted the outside. Still don't know how Mama convinced Mr. Anthony to get involved.

Occasionally, a twinge of guilt rises up and I feel a little sorry for the drunk mama. Doesn't last long though, then I'm back plotting ways to get rid of her. My latest plan involves bus money and a trip to Alaska. Mama on the other hand, plans for us all to live happily ever after as one big family.

"Hey, there's a giant turtle with a fat baby riding on his back."

I scoot to the center of the blanket. "Where?"

"Right there, you see the baby's foot hanging down?"

I squint and look harder. "Can't see anything but clouds today." I sit up and look down at Sam. Her face is one big smile. "You want to make clover necklaces?"

"Nah," she says, still staring at the sky. "Maybe it's an angel, no, it's a baby all right, no wings."

I yank a clover from the ground and count the leaves. Three. "We could go visit Bea."

Sam sits up, touches a finger to the pink scar on her forehead. "Ya know your Mama is planning a party to celebrate your birthday."

"Uh-huh, she told me," I say without enthusiasm. "Said Bea and your mama are invited. That should make an interesting party."

"She's doing better. Got a job running the register over at the café, might even get to wait tables soon." Her eyes are on my face. "Maggie, I need to tell you something, but you gotta promise not to get mad."

"Go ahead."

"First promise," she says.

Sliding my hand behind my back, I cross my fingers and say, "Promise."

She looks away. "I'm going home," she says softly.

I wait for her to laugh. I wait. Finally, she looks at me and I know. "Sam, you can't. I'm going to tell Daddy, he won't let you go back."

"He already knows. It'll be all right, Maggie, she can't drink around me."

"Who's going to keep that from happening?"

She ignores the question. "I've got a good feeling. This time's gonna be different. Please try and understand."

I reach over, brush tears from her cheeks, then lay back on the blanket. "When you going?"

"I'll go home with her after your party." She grabs my hand. "You see the cloud baby?'

"Yeah, I see it now." ❧

⤳ TWENTY-FOUR ⤳

I USUALLY CAN'T WAIT for August eleventh to arrive. Two years ago, I begged Daddy to pretend my birth was on July twenty-fifth. Told him I couldn't bear to put it off another day, so we celebrated twice that year. Now, I want to skip the entire thing. Mama's been up the last two nights, baking and cleaning. She says she's fine, just busy, but sleepless nights are never a good sign. Daddy's pretend smile has been plastered across his face all morning and Sam's clothes are back in her brown paper sack.

"Mama, I'm not feeling too good," I say, walking into the kitchen. I rub my head and try to look pale. "We might need to cancel the party."

"Is it your stomach?" She touches my forehead. "No fever. You're just excited is all. Frank, go outside and help Samantha with the balloons. She's having a time getting them to stay put on the picnic table. Mags, honey, go rest. I'll let you know when your guests arrive. It's going to be a great party. I've even cooked your favorite supper - baked chicken."

I fight the urge to fake a seizure and walk to my room.

Daddy follows me, grabbing the door before it slams shut. "Mags, you all right?"

"Since when is baked chicken my favorite supper?"

"Well, you don't hate it, do you?" He leans against the wall.

"Guess not," I say.

"You might enjoy the party."

"Why did she have to invite Sam's mama? Shouldn't I at least like the people at my party?"

"Maybe Colleen won't come." He runs his hand through his hair, smoothing back the stubborn pieces.

I look away and stare at the wall. "Mama's getting sick again, huh?"

"Yes."

"Do you think it's from spending so much time with Sam's mama?" I ask.

"I doubt it. Just something that happens."

"When did it start?"

"A few weeks ago. She hasn't been sleeping much, cries a lot at night, the usual. Seems to be coming on faster this time, though."

"I should have noticed. I'm sorry, Daddy."

"Maggie, there's nothing you could have done. Anyway, I think she may pull out of it this time." He moves to the door. "Better go help Samantha with those balloons. Wanna give us a hand?"

"Need to change clothes first."

"Don't take too long. You don't want to miss your party." He smiles and closes the door.

I move to the window. "Lord, how did I not notice?" I don't have to wait until heaven to know the answer to this one. In my world of sisters and poetry, there just wasn't room for a sick mama.

Ten minutes after the guests arrive, I walk to the kitchen wearing my special occasion dress; the emerald green one with a white lace collar and sash. The one that would never get worn if it wasn't Mama's favorite.

"Maggie, you look beautiful. Doesn't she look beautiful, Frank?"

Daddy slips his arm around Mama's waist. "Sure does. Happy birthday, Mags."

Mama smiles and it's hard to believe she's not anything but perfect. "Colleen, Bea and Samantha are out back. Do you want to eat cake first or open the presents?"

"What do you think?" I ask.

She moves to my side and slips her hand over mine. "Presents first, I can't wait another minute to see what you've gotten." She leads me out the back door. "Well, what do you think?"

Bea, Sam, the drunk mama, and a three-layered cake surrounded by a sea of blue, red and yellow balloons look as if they need rescuing. Some purple and green ones have floated to the ground, while more of the red and yellow ones dangle from the pine tree. The decorations, along with a hat the size of Miss Clark's porch resting on Bea's head, Sam's construction paper party hat compete with a red balloon, and the drunk mama stuck between the two, causes me to laugh out loud.

Sam frowns. "You don't like it," she says softly.

"No, the decorations look great."

She smiles her Christmas morning grin. "Bea made the cake."

Bea shoves a balloon away from the cake. "It's my Strawberry Delight. There's fresh strawberries mixed right into the batter."

"Thanks, Bea; I know it will be delicious."

Daddy grabs my hand, "Come on, let's get started."

Mama takes the spot on one end; Daddy slides in across from Bea, leaving me the middle. I glare at the drunk mama, who looks as if she may jump under the table and crawl away. Reckon its hard being at a party with no alcohol.

"Maggie, open your presents," Sam says.

I search the table but find nothing but balloons. "Where are they?"

Sam giggles. "Oh, I forgot. Put them under the table cause they wouldn't fit on top." She disappears and returns with a box wrapped with yellow ribbon. "Open mine first."

I remove the top and look down at a rag doll dressed in a blue gingham dress and white apron. "She's beautiful, Sam."

"I made her, well, Bea helped a bunch. Look on the apron. See what's embroidered on the bottom?"

I lift the doll from the box and look closely at the blue stitching. "Sisters forever," I say softly.

"I've got one too. That way we'll never forget each other."

"I love her red hair."

"She's supposed to be me. Mine has brown hair like you. She's at Mama's since I'm going home today, but I'll bring her over to show you."

Suddenly, my face is on fire and I'm overwhelmed with a desire to run. Bea reaches over and squeezes my hand. Her smile keeps me from leaving the table, squawking like a baby.

"Mine next," she says. "Samantha, get the one with the pink bow."

I open the box, dig through mounds of the *Pearl Gazette*, to find a white apron with my name stitched along the bottom. Nestled underneath are pages of handwritten recipes.

"Now you can't give those out to nobody. Those are top secret, only you and your mama, and maybe Samantha can use 'em. Don't even let Mr. Frank see. You gotta promise me, now, or I'll have to take 'em back."

"I'll guard them with my life," I say, smiling.

"If you need help the first time, come to me. There's an art to baking cookies, you know."

I nod as Sam sticks a paper sack in my hands. I peek in and grin. "Where did y'all find these?"

"That's not from us," Daddy says.

The drunk mama clears her throat. "Um-m, those are from me. Found 'em in Carlson. Samantha said you love books on California. Hope you don't already have those two."

Keeping my eyes on the books, I say, "No, I, uh, thank you."

"Colleen, that was so kind of you to go all the way to Carlson. Wasn't that thoughtful, Maggie?"

I glance at Mama. "Yes, ma'am, it was." Again, I have the urge to run.

"All right, here's the last one."

I take a small box from Sam and rip through the paper to find a silver bracelet. "Mama, I can't believe y'all got me this! Look, Sam, isn't it beautiful?"

"Your daddy picked out the book charm, and I choose the heart. Every time you look at it I want you to remember how much we love you."

"And the little folding chair?" I ask.

Daddy smiles. "We both picked that one."

"So you won't forget our beach and the fun we had that day," Mama says.

"Mama, help me put it on."

"Let your daddy, I need to run inside for a minute. Bea, would you please cut the cake." Before anyone can respond, Mama's halfway to the back door.

"I need to check on Elizabeth, y'all go ahead and eat the cake." Daddy almost runs to the house, leaving me to stare at the charm bracelet.

"Here, child, I'll put it on you." Bea struggles off the bench and walks around the table. "Now, then, looks right pretty hanging there on your wrist. Yes sir, that's a mighty fine gift." She digs through balloons to find the knife and paper plates, and serves each of us a large chunk. With a piece in her mouth, she mumbles, "Don't mean to brag none, but this here's one of my best."

We all agree, and eat while Sam rambles about the cake, my presents and the table decorations. Someone listening would think it was her birthday party. I smile and stare at the screen door. Finally, Daddy walks back out.

"The coffee's ready. Who wants a cup?"

Bea stands, straightens her dress and looks my way. "I need to be going, got work to do. Thanks for the invite." She tilts the brim of the hat back so I can see her face. "Happy birthday, Maggie."

I hop up and throw my arms around her waist. "Thanks, Bea."

"It's been my pleasure. Now remember, top secret."

"Bea, let me drive you home," Daddy says.

"Oh, no, Mr. Frank, I'm chugged full of cake. The walk will do me good," she says, waddling across the yard.

"Colleen, go join Elizabeth on the front porch. Maggie will bring the coffee out."

I don't move. She was nice to give me those books, but I'd rather scrub the kitchen floor than serve her coffee. Besides, she's probably just pretending to be nice. Her true, drunk self will show up sooner or later.

"Maggie, don't just stand there, go fix the coffee. Samantha, will you help me clean the table?"

"Sure, Mr. Frank, but can we leave the balloons? They look so pretty."

"Don't see why not."

I want to argue that it's my birthday, so Sam should have to serve the coffee. I want to stomp my feet and beg, but instead take a deep breath and shuffle to the kitchen. After all,

I am twelve years old now. The silver tray's on the counter with Mama's blue and white china cups, matching sugar bowl and creamer perched on top. Voices drift in through the window. I move to the living room, crouch below the windowsill, and listen. The porch swing creaks into motion. I peek out, just enough to see.

"Do you mind?" Colleen says, pulling a pack of cigarettes from her pocket. She sticks one in her mouth and tries to strike a match.

"Lord," I whisper, "her hand's shaking so bad, don't let her catch the porch on fire."

As if prompted by Jesus himself, Mama eases the match from her hand and smiles. "Let me do that."

After a few puffs, the drunk mama closes her eyes. "Some days are harder than others."

"We have to make the best of the good ones, and just get through the bad ones. You know, we're alike, you and I."

The drunk mama's foot slams the swing to a stop. "You ain't nothing like me."

"We both hurt the ones we love."

She stares at Mama for what seems hours, then says, "Don't you think I know Samantha deserves better?"

The swing creaks back into motion. "Both our girls deserve better. Sometimes we have to do what's best for them, even if we get hurt. Samantha loves you and wants to give it another chance, and I pray it works, but always know that she can live here."

"Is it selfish for me to take her home?"

"No more selfish than what I do to my family."

She tosses the half-smoked cigarette into the yard, and closes her eyes again. "I'm scared, either way; I'm scared half to death."

I move away as Mama's arm goes around the drunk mama's shoulder. "You're nothing like her," I say to the empty kitchen.

Daddy walks through the back door, cake in hand. "What'd you say?"

"Nothing, getting the coffee is all."

"I'll pour me a cup and meet y'all outside. Samantha's just about done."

I fill the cups and walk slowly to the swing. "Here you go, watch out it's hot."

"Thank you, Mags." Mama places the tray on the small table beside the swing. She adds cream to one cup and serves the other black.

I turn to leave but stop. "Uh, Miss Colleen, thanks for coming. I really like the books."

"I'm glad," she says softly.

"Maggie," Mama says, "would you like to join us?"

Before I can answer, Daddy comes through the screen door, mug in hand. He eases down by the swing, grabbing Mama's foot with his empty hand. Sam arrives next with milk and moon pies. We sit on the steps and make milk moustaches while our mamas talk. When our glasses our nearly empty Sam leans in and whispers, "keep eating the moon pies. I've got little mosquito bites now too, must be working."

I take a bite of the yellow pie, thankful for a miracle, and settle into the step. We talk about the upcoming election, agreeing it's time for a new mayor. Daddy brings up the missing Alcatraz convicts, which leads to a long discussion of whether they're dead or alive. The sun slides behind the oak tree and we complain about the heat. Sam says she's looking forward to fall, but not school. Daddy's eyes seldom leave Mama's face; the sparkle returning a bit every time she laughs. We talk, and as fireflies dart around the yard, Colleen begins to look a little like the woman in Sam's buried photographs. ⌒

~(TWENTY-FIVE)~

WITH THE LAST plate washed, dried and in the cabinet I join Mama on the sofa. "The chicken was good. I'm glad Sam and her mama stayed for supper."

"Me too," Mama says.

"Daddy should be back soon from taking them home. You wanna watch the news or something?"

"If you don't mind, I like the quiet." She leans back and closes her eyes.

I run my finger along a circle imprinted on her temple. "Mama, what's this?"

She looks at me for a moment, and then closes her eyes again. "It's from the shock treatments. That's where they hook the wires."

"Are you awake during the treatments?" I ask, then immediately want to take it back.

"Until the electricity knocks me out," she says.

I look away. "Oh."

Mama takes my hand. "Maggie, you know I love you and your daddy more than anything."

"Yes ma'am."

"I'd give anything to stay with you, to never leave. You know that, don't you?"

"Yes ma'am."

"Don't ever forget how much I love you."

I take a deep breath. "Mama, you can remind me every day, that way I won't forget."

"I won't always be here, so you have to remember." She sits up, kisses my forehead and smiles. "Think I'll turn in."

"Why don't you wait for Daddy? He'll be home soon."

"Wait for what?" a voice says from the door.

"Daddy, I didn't hear you drive up."

"Had the truck in silent mode," he laughs. "What are you two doing?"

Mama stands. "Frank, I'm going to bed. It's been a long day," she says and walks out the room.

"Mags, you want to play some cards?"

"No thanks, I'm beat. It was a real nice party." I move toward the kitchen. "Daddy, maybe you should go on to bed yourself. Mama may need something."

When I'm in bed he stops at my bedroom door and asks, "Lights on or off?"

"Off," I say. When the door closes I slip to the floor and kneel. "Lord," I whisper, "keep her safe. Amen."

It's close to midnight when I climb from bed and feel my way to the kitchen. I slide my hand along the counter, careful not to knock over the salt and pepper shakers, and switch on the lamp. All three are shaped like roosters, bought two weeks earlier along with a ceramic cookie jar complete with a chicken's head.

"Maggie?"

I twirl around to face the table. "Mama you scared me! Why are you sitting in the dark?"

"Couldn't sleep," she mumbles.

"Me neither. Woke up wanting another piece of Bea's cake." I watch Mama fiddle with something in her lap. "What ya got?" I lean over to get a better look. Her fingers tighten around the medicine bottle. My eyes move to the blank stare on her face. "You want a glass of milk and cake?"

"You know I can't do that," she whispers. "That's how they control your mind."

I ease the bottle from her hand. "Mama, you don't need that right now. I'll put it up." I stick the bottle in the pocket of my gown, and grab her hand. "Come on, you can sleep with me."

"Maggie," she says climbing into bed beside me, "don't let them inside your head. That's the beginning you know."

I wait until she's asleep, and then slip out to the living room. I grab the quilt from the chair, curl up on the couch, and fall asleep searching my mind for missed clues.

"Maggie, why aren't you in bed?"

I peek out from under the quilt and mumble, "Is it morning?"

Daddy brushes hair from my eyes. "Yeah, early though. What are you doing in here?"

"She's getting worse." I sit up, to make room for him, but, he turns and walks into the kitchen. I follow and lean against the stove as he fills his Thermos. "Save me some," I say.

He glances my direction. "Since when do you drink coffee?"

"I'm twelve now, that's old enough." I sit at the table and wait for the hundred reasons why I can't have a cup.

Instead, he grabs two mugs, fills both with steaming, black coffee and places them on the table. "Sugar and milk?"

I nod, shocked by the ease of victory. "Are you feeling all right?" I ask.

He sits across from me. "You've earned the right. Be careful, it's hot."

I quickly stir in sugar and milk and take a gulp. I blink as the hot liquid enters my mouth and burns its way down my throat. "Tastes good," I lie.

Daddy smiles, "Now, don't drink more than a pot a day."

"Yeah, all right," I say and take a much smaller sip. "Daddy, she's getting worse."

His smile fades. "I'm meeting with her doctor this afternoon. She refuses to go, says he's the antichrist." The chair scraps across the linoleum as he stands. "She's really having trouble keeping her thoughts right, so if you need to, go to the Clarks'. I'll be home early. Good thing I didn't take that foreman job." He kisses the top of my head, grabs the thermos and walks out the door.

Most of the morning is spent trying to get Mama out of bed. Finally, I give up and crawl in beside her. "Mama, you want me to read from your poetry books? That one about the whippoorwill's nice."

"Lies, all lies," she mumbles.

"How 'bout some food? I'll serve you in bed this time."

She turns away and whispers, "No, no, poison."

A familiar sadness fills me then like a night with no stars. Don't know why, but even with all the prayers and high hopes, we're right back in that same starless place. This is one thing I wish God would explain before heaven. Not knowing why can gnaw a hole right through a person. I've tried my hardest to find the answer. Back in Minden, I listened to almost every word out of Brother Jim's mouth, did my best to pay attention in Sunday School, and even attended Vacation Bible School three summers in a row, but still no answer.

Maybe I'm not to question why. Just suppose to pick up my cross, sing *Amazing Grace*, and let the weight of things build character. Bea's cross carrying theory makes sense for someone like me, but Mama has more character than any person I know. She should be cross free or at least given a smaller one. Wonder if there is a committee of angels up there deciding who gets what cross? If so, when I get to heaven, their meeting is where I'll head right after my question and answer session with God.

I leave Mama chanting about poison and walk to the kitchen. The coffee pot, still on the stove, has a cup or two left, but no longer holds my interest. I move to the sink and gaze out at the beach. Green patches peak through the sand, brown leaves float in the pool and the Golden Gate Bridge lies face down on the ground. My mind wanders to Alcatraz and the three missing men. How long did it take to dig through concrete with spoons? Then, after all that, they plunge into the bay not knowing if they'd make it to land or drown. Not having answers didn't make them give up. I swear if they weren't bandits, I'd want their autographs.

I grab an apple, cut it into four pieces and walk back to my room. Taking a bite, I say, "Look, it's not poison."

Mama stops mumbling long enough to eat the apple and I walk from the room feeling like I just dug through a wall.

That evening, Daddy finds me scooping leaves from the pool. He watches for a moment, then says, "Sorry, I'm so late. Planning to take a dip?"

"No sir just wanted to get the beach in order."

He leans over and grabs a handful of leaves. "Went by Samantha and Colleen's on my way home. They're both doing good."

"Yeah?"

"We're keeping a close eye on them, so don't you worry."

"Hope Sam has sense enough to run if her mama starts drinking."

"She will, Mags. How's your day been?"

I smile. "Got Mama to eat an apple."

He stares at the ground, then turns away. "Need to change clothes," he says, as the screen door slams shut.

I stare at the closed door and wonder why he isn't impressed by our great accomplishment. He's probably dehydrated. Never knew a man more determined not to drink water. I finish the pool, straighten the bridge, and head inside. I fill a glass with water and find Daddy in the hall watching Mama sleep.

"Here, bet you haven't had a drop all day."

"Wish things were different for you, Maggie."

"Daddy, you know she'll get well again, she always does."

He takes the glass and smiles. "I met with a new doctor today. He's young, fresh out of medical school. Says he's fascinated with your mama's case and wants to try a new medicine."

"You like him?"

"Well, he's a real confident fellow. It'll take a few visits with your mama to find out what he's made of. He'll either rise to the challenge or run for the hills."

I take a deep breath, thankful for the never-ending supply of doctors. No matter, good or bad, each brings the possibility of life without the illness.

"How 'bout we play a few games of Monopoly before bed?"

"I'm the hat, no, the dog, tonight," I say.

He smiles. "Let's go set up the game."

For the next few hours, the worst thing in life is landing on Park Avenue without enough money to make a purchase. We circle the board, buy property and go in and out of jail, promising just one more game after each win. Finally, close to midnight, we fold the board, stack the money and say goodnight. ⌒

~⟨ TWENTY-SIX ⟩~

NIGHT-TIME NOISES DRIFT through the open window and I listen for what woke me. I make my way through the familiar noises, branches brushing the side of the house, the barn owl in the oak out back, and settle on a sound inside my room. I search the dark and wish, for the second time in my life, to have super powers. This time I need night vision. While the wish dangles in my mind, the moon moves from behind a cloud, leaking small rays of light across the room. My eyes focus on someone by the bed.

"Mama?"

In the dim light she looks like a ghost from a Dickens story: pale skin, white flowing gown, hands shaking their way back and forth across her body. Her mouth opens and words rush out in an unknown melody.

"Coming for you, coming for you," she sings. "You'll be gone. We'll all be gone." The song continues as she floats out the room and down the hall.

When the words fade, I throw a dress over my nightshirt, and climb out the window. I head down the gravel drive, stopping every few feet to reconsider. After all, no one's coming. Mama's just having one of her delusions, or hallucinations, or whatever fancy word describes this situation. I think of Daddy and want to turn back, but the banging in my chest keeps me moving. When my feet hit Clark Road, I take out in a run and don't stop until I'm twenty feet from the house.

"Lord," I whisper, "sure hope they're not light sleepers. Hate to be taken for a robber." All at once, the moon glides behind a cloud, and I'm wrapped in total darkness. I stare up into the starless sky. "Don't know if that was you, but thanks just in case. Nice to know you don't want me shot dead right here in the yard."

I creep to the back porch and tap on the side door. It creaks open.

"Maggie, child, what's wrong?"

I stare for a moment, searching for a believable story. "I, uh, had a nightmare."

"Your folks know where you are?"

I shake my head no. "Didn't want to wake them. If it's too much of a bother, I'll go back home."

Bea stands aside. "No bother, come in."

For all the time I've spent at the Clarks', this is my first time in Bea's room. She motions toward the twin bed squeezed between a rocker and a small dresser. A photograph of an old colored woman and Bible are on the windowsill.

"Why you dressed in the middle of the night?" I ask.

"It's four o'clock."

"Well, that's still the night."

"Not for me. I get up this early every day, been doing it for years. Gives me time for scripture readin' and a talk with the Lord." She smiles. "Go head, child, it's still the middle of the night to you. Get some sleep."

"I probably need to go home, they'll be worried."

"At daylight, I'll call and let 'em know where you are. Go on now, you're about to fall asleep standing there."

Suddenly exhausted, I lay across the bed. "Don't forget to call Daddy."

"Don't you worry none, honey." She reaches over and gives my head a pat, like one might give a stray puppy. I don't mind, though, seeing how she's probably never put either a dog or girl to bed before. She pats a few more times, then sits in the rocker and bows her head.

I wake to an empty room and want nothing more than to hide in bed all day. There's going to be some explaining to do and right now I can't explain to my own self what happened. Daddy will see right through my nightmare excuse. He'll probably nail my window shut, or make me sleep on the floor in his bedroom for the next fifteen years. I push open the red checked curtains and the urge to say in bed grows. There's not a spec of blue in the sky, just gray every which way, the sun no where to be found. If I didn't know better, I'd think winter crept in last night. The door opens, right before I pull the sheet over my head.

"You're awake, good. Got bacon, buttermilk biscuits and molasses warming on the stove. You hungry?" Bea smiles, like it's a regular day.

"Thanks, but I'd better get home."

"Your daddy wants you to stay here. He's working a few hours, then he's gonna take your mama to the doctor. He'll pick you up after."

"Oh," I say.

"Come on, now, you need to eat breakfast before supper time. Besides, Samantha will be here soon to get the surprise."

"What surprise?"

"Mr. Anthony got it for her."

"What it is?" I ask, following Bea across the porch. "Why did he get her a present? It's not her birthday. What does Miss Clark think about all of this? I'll bet she's not too happy, since she claims Sam's the spawn of Satan."

Bea stops at the back door. "I do declare, you sure talk a lot for someone right out of bed."

I reach up, brush a blotch of white powder from her face, and smile. "You sure do make a mess cooking."

"Yeah, well, biscuit makin's a messy business."

The door opens and I'm hit with the scent of bacon, cinnamon and vanilla. I hurry to the kitchen table, suddenly realizing I'm about to starve to death. "What cookies are you baking?"

"Oatmeal, which I believe, is your favorite." Bea slides my plate and a jar of molasses on the table.

"But it's chocolate chip day."

"It is my cookie schedule." She leans against the counter and watches me stuff the second biscuit into my mouth. "Slow down, child, you're going to choke yourself."

I nod and reach for the bacon. "What's the surprise?"

"Land's sake, Maggie, ain't lady like to talk with your mouth full." She plops another biscuit on my plate and pours a puddle of molasses next to it. "Mr. Anthony went and bought her a brand new bicycle, red as ole man Crawford's wagon."

I swallow. "For Sam?"

"Yeah, don't know what he was thinking bringing it here. Miss Clark threw a good one." Bea dabs her face with a handkerchief. "He usually gives in, but not this time. Told her flat out he wasn't turning his back on Samantha. Said if she didn't like it, he'd leave."

"Ever since Sam got out the hospital he's been acting concerned. Why the sudden interest now?"

"Not my place to say."

"How am I supposed to find out then?"

Bea shrugs and walks to the sink. "Dunno, but it won't come from me."

"What if I guess? You can just nod your head to let me know if I'm right."

"No child, I gave my word."

Bea's word is better than any blood promise. It'd be easier to get information from a communist spy. I sigh as loud as humanly possible then take a bite of molasses dipped biscuit.

"You want to see the bicycle?"

"I'll wait for Sam. Think I'll bring Mama some breakfast."

"Your daddy said to wait here. He'll be home shortly."

"Mama needs to eat something. I'll be right back."

"Well, I reckon, but don't make me come get you."

Bea's stern look and tough talk makes me smile. "What ya gonna do?"

"I'll get a switch off the mulberry bush and spank you good."

I laugh. "You'd have to catch me first."

She wraps bacon and two biscuits in a dishrag. "Don't be gone long, you hear?"

"Promise," I say walking to the kitchen door. "Thanks, Bea." ❧

~(TWENTY-SEVEN)~

ALFWAY HOME, A heaviness climbs on my shoulders causing me to stop in the middle of Clark Road. Don't know why Daddy wanted me to stay with Bea, but then, after last night, he's probably scared I'm crazy and need supervision. I look up at the sky. "Lord, don't you think this has gone on long enough? Brother Jim says everything in life, no matter how bad, can be good for us. Says, you'll use it to make us better people. Well, as far as I can see Mama and Daddy are just about as good as they can get. There are lots people who are down right mean. Why don't you concentrate on them for awhile?" I take a deep breath. "Lord, please get her well for good. They can't take much more of this."

I know better than to wait for an answer, besides, talking to God in the middle of the road isn't a good idea. Cars seldom travel Clark Road, but the way my luck's been, a caravan will turn the curve any minute now. If anyone sees me, I'll be the talk of Sunshine. I walk across the street, then jog to our driveway, making it to the house unseen by any of Pearl's fine, tongue wagging citizens.

"Mama, brought you something to eat," I call out. Before the door closes behind me, the biscuits hit the floor as I look around at the minefield that was our living room. Blue and white china lay in pieces across the floor, a cracked mirror leans against the wall, and two circles made from large chunks of clear glass are covered with the same red as the footprints leading in and out of the room. The grandfather clock, along with the television screen have been smashed. There are bits of wood and glass in small piles around the room. "I know what you are trying to do," written in red lipstick, sprawls across the wall.

I stand, unable to move, and listen to the pounding of my heart. "Mama," I whisper, "you there?" She comes from behind the sofa, Daddy's plaid shirt wrapped around her shoulders. "Mama, your feet are bleeding! You need to be still. Mama, don't walk on the glass."

"Did they follow you? Did they see you come inside?" Her voice is high and unfamiliar.

"Mama, I'm gonna go back to Bea's. I'll get Daddy."

She moves quickly across the floor, crouches beside me and yanks my arm. I land between two large pieces of clear glass and stare at the knife in her left hand.

"We could both go to Bea's. Would you like that?"

She sits, eyes never leaving the window, and wraps her arm around my waist. "They came last night and I begged them not to take you. They're coming back."

"Let me go get Daddy. He'll keep us safe."

"No! He works for them." She pulls me closer. "The devices are gone, they can't hear us now."

"Mama, please let me . . ."

"Sh-h-h, hush now, no talking." Words become jumbled, then turn into a soft hum. My head drifts to her shoulder, eyes close as I force my mind to a night, two years earlier.

❧

I closed the book, wished for a better flashlight and wondered if this was a mistake. The dim lit tent felt safe enough, but what if a wild animal came from the woods? Maybe I shouldn't have begged. Actually, Mama's kiss had convinced Daddy to agree. I cradled the flashlight in my arms and listened. The wind rustled the top of the tent and an animal, perhaps a wild, hungry wolf, called out in the distance. I sat up, ready to fight.

"Mags, you still awake?"

I sucked in air, "Mama?"

She crawled inside with the picnic basket. "Hey, brought you a snack. You know, since there are no coconut trees or wild fruit growing nearby."

I peeked in and grabbed an apple. "What time is it?"

"Almost midnight." Mama watched me for a moment, then pulled out some grapes. "I've always wanted to sleep outside. I know you want to be alone, but it would mean a lot if I could stay. Would you mind?"

I didn't answer right away, pretending to make a sacrifice. I made sure not to smile and said, "Well, if it's that important to you."

Mama squeezed my hand. "Thanks, Maggie. You're so brave to stay out here alone. I'd be too afraid."

I took a bite of apple, ready to confess, when suddenly the tent lit up. We both yelled, "turn off the porch light."

Daddy laughed and it was dark again. Footsteps were followed by another body in the tent. "It's lonely in the house."

We scooted around until everyone was comfortable. "I'd still rather be living on an island," I said.

Daddy moaned, "Not again. Aren't you ready for a new book? You've read that one three times."

The Island of the Blue Dolphins *turned into a spear as I poked his belly.* "Just about."

"Good." *Daddy smiled, stretched out beside Mama, and said,* "Good-night, girls."

She laid her head in the crook of his arm and said, "Love y'all."

I laid back and switched off the light. "Thanks for letting me sleep in the tent." *I moved my leg until it touched Mama's, then closed my eyes.*

❧

My body aches from sitting in one position so long, but I don't dare move. Her eyes are closed; head folded forward, the knife on the floor by her hand. I take a deep breath, then let the air escape slowly through my mouth, something Daddy taught me when I had to give an oral report in fifth grade. I breathe in again, this time, eyes closed. With air still in my lungs, mama moves, and puts an end to Daddy's calming trick.

She looks around the room, then whispers, "We need to leave."

"No, we'll stay here." My words trickle out more a plea, than a command.

"You're working with them!" In one motion, she grabs the knife and stands.

"No, I'm not, I promise." Tears run down my face as she pulls my arm. "Mama, let go, you're hurting me."

The knife slides beside my face as an order to stand comes from a woman that is no longer my mama.

I lose all track of time, not sure if we've been in our new position five minutes or five hours. Mama's latest strategy to fight finds us on the couch with a clear view of the door.

She alternates from hurling curse words across the room, to crying uncontrollable. Occasionally, she waves the knife through the air, and speaks to people I can't see.

The door vibrates and a muffled voice demands it to open, sending Mama into motion. She slips to the floor, knife in hand, and positions herself in front of my legs, crouched, ready for battle.

"I'm coming in!"

Mama whispers, "Don't worry, it will be over soon."

The door opens and I stare at a stranger with a gun. He looks like one of those junior high boys who roam in packs pretending to be seniors; the ones with bad complexions and voices belonging to freshman girls. Today, he's a sheriff. A blue cap hides his eyes, but from the way the gun shakes in his hand, I know they are filled with fear. I ease to the edge of the couch and slip my hand on Mama's shoulder. Her body stiffens and a moan from a trapped animal escapes her lips.

"Ma'am, I need you to put the knife down. You have to the count of ten to lower the knife."

Count of ten, then what? In my mind, I slide down beside Mama, ease the knife from her hand, and tell this boy to go home. I see this, but can't make my body move.

"One, two . . ."

I beg my body to cooperate, will it to move, but nothing, as if it is no longer mine to control.

"Three, four . . ."

Mama presses back into my legs, raises the knife and yells, "You can't have her!"

"Put the knife down! Put it down right now!"

"Stay away!"

"I don't wanna have to shoot you!"

Hands fly up, covering my ears, as the two of them shout back and forth, their voices sounding more desperate with each response. I suck air through a straw like throat, squeeze my eyes close, and wait for my heart to pound its way through my chest. I wait, until a voice, soft and calm, penetrates the screams. I breathe; Daddy's here.

"Elizabeth, put the knife down."

"Sir, you need to leave. Sir, step outside!"

"Elizabeth, I need you to give me the knife." Daddy steps in front of the boy, making him curse under his breath and move to get a clear view of the couch.

"I can't go back, no, no, can't go back," Mama sobs.

Daddy moves to the right, again blocking the sheriff's view. "It's all right, Elizabeth you're safe. Please, give me the knife."

No one else would notice the change in his voice, or the way the words shook themselves free, slow and careful. His creased brow, the straight line for lips, and the slight tremor of his hands, would also go unseen, hidden by the certainty of his steps. Knowing he can't take much more, I lean toward Mama. I get close so she'll listen, but before I speak, she twists around and the knife is once again pointing toward my face.

"Maggie, move back!"

Daddy leaps forward, pushes my body against the couch with one arm and grabs Mama with the other. She screams as he twists her arm until the knife falls to the ground. Hands crash against his chest and curse words fly into his face, but he stands, shielding me from the illness. Finally, when she collapses into his body, he lifts her into his arms. The sheriff moves toward them, but stops when Daddy motions my way. Instead he follows them outside, gun still drawn.

Seconds later Bea rushes in and crosses the room in three strides. She sits, pulls me to her chest and whispers, "Sweet Jesus, sweet Jesus," over and over.

When Daddy walks in, I'm still wrapped in her arms, face buried in the soft folds of her dress. Bea releases her grip and I move my face from her shoulder. With eyes, swollen almost shut, I watch Daddy kneel in front of the couch.

"Mags, honey are you all right? Are you hurt?" He examines one foot at a time, then checks my arms and hands.

"I'm fine."

"Mr. Frank, Maggie can stay with me while you go to the hospital and check on Miss Elizabeth."

He lifts me from the couch and I am five again, head down, face pressed into the curve of his neck. The knot in my belly begins to unravel, and for the first time since entering the house, my hands are still. He walks to the door, and without looking back says, "Not going to the hospital."

We leave the door wide open; Bea on the couch, hands pressed together, head bent forward, eyes closed. He carries me to the truck and I slide over just enough for him to fit behind the wheel. Neither of us speak until we're half-way to Carlson.

"Daddy, where did he take Mama?"

"Wakefield."

I scoot to the middle of the seat. "Don't you need to make sure she gets there all right?"

"She'll be fine."

"Where are we going?"

He looks at me and answers so low I barely hear the words, "I don't know."

∾∾

I grab the fender, squat and pray pee doesn't splash against my legs. At least I don't have to worry about being seen, there's been no sign of life for miles. I fell asleep right outside of Carlson, and woke in wilderness, nothing but pine trees and black top. Doesn't seem important to know where we are, which is good, because I honestly don't think Daddy has a clue. I step over the puddle, walk to the passenger door and climb in as the engine sputters to life.

"Your peanuts and Coke are in the bag."

"Thanks," I say, ignoring the paper sack. "Daddy, aren't you tired?"

"I'm fine. You go on back to sleep."

The gear grinds and we're once again speeding through the dark to nowhere. ᴥ

~ TWENTY-EIGHT ~

S UNLIGHT IS THE first thing I notice; the second is that
I'm alone. I spring up, mouth open to scream, when
I see the tree house. I jump from the truck and run
inside ready to tip through broken glass. To my surprise
there is none.

"Daddy?"

"In here."

He's at the kitchen table, hands around the only glass still
in one piece. "When did we get home?" I ask.

"Little before sunrise. I didn't want to wake you." He at-
tempts a smile, then looks away. "Maggie, I've been thinking
about how much you want to live in San Francisco. I should be
able to find work there."

"Really? You want to move to California? Thought you
didn't like big cities."

His eyes move from the floor, to the glass. "Yeah, well, it
might be nice to live by the ocean."

I give him a quick hug, then dance around the kitchen. "I can't believe this! Sam will have to move with us, even if Colleen has to tag along. Wish Bea could come too. Maybe she can work for us, don't think Miss Clark treats her all that nice, so she'd probably love the opportunity to leave. I'm sure there are good hospitals there. Probably have better doctors, too. Mama will love living near the beach, don't you think?"

He takes a sip of water, then says, "Your Mama won't be going."

"What do you mean?"

"It'll be better if she stays here."

"Oh, until she gets well? That makes sense. Maybe once we're settled, she can transfer to a hospital over there. Don't you think she'll be well enough, by then, Daddy?"

"She won't move with us." He clears his throat, then adds, "Mags, we can start fresh, a brand new life."

"No! What's wrong with you? We can't leave Mama." He grabs my hand, but I pull away. "I won't go!"

"Maggie, this is what your mama wants."

"That's not true! She would never want me to leave her. Daddy she was just confused. Please, let's just stay here. I like Pearl, now. Besides, school begins in a few weeks." I lean against the counter. "Daddy, I won't go."

"This is not your decision to make!" Unfamiliar, purple veins pop out along his neck as he grasps for air. "You don't know what's best! Nothing like this can ever happen again!" His fist slams down so quick, I almost jump out of my skin. The glass falls from the table spraying the floor with glass and water.

"Daddy!"

He reaches for my hand, but I move back against the counter. I stare at the pool forming by Daddy's feet and wish to have the day at Mama's beach back.

"Maggie, honey, I'm so sorry."

I look at his face: the deep line etched between his brow, the dark shadows under both eyes, and I'm struck with a thought that breaks my heart. I whisper, "She doesn't want us to leave, you just don't love her anymore."

His breath catches in the back of his throat as he slumps forward. "I will always love your mama."

I blink back tears. "Then why do want to leave her here?"

"Can't you understand that we owe you something better?"

"Moving without Mama is not better." I slip my hand in his. "Yesterday was my fault. I should have listened to you and stayed with Bea. From now on, when she gets sick, I'll go to the Clarks' or stay outside. I'll do whatever you say, Daddy, just please don't make me leave her."

He closes his eyes and doesn't move. My eyes drift around the room. The small dish used to hold Mama's rings no longer sits by the sink; two apples are on the counter instead of in the flowered bowl she bought at a thrift store in Redding; the turkey platter transformed to hold moon pies, gone. I scan the counter between the stove and refrigerator and stop. There, stuck in the corner, is the lamp with the salt and pepper shakers perched on either side. I'm suddenly filled with an urge to run over and kiss their ugly beaks, which makes no sense at all. Never cared much for the matching set of roosters, but seeing them in one piece fills me with hope. I glance over at Daddy who is awake and staring at me. His lips curl into a half smile.

"Daddy?"

"We don't deserve you, Mags."

"Does this mean we're not leaving?"

"Don't think I could have really gone through with it. I can't be that far away from your mama." He shakes his head and looks down at the stream of water and broken glass. "Now, I suppose we need to clean up this water. Can't believe I managed to break the only glass left in the house."

"Wait here, I just remembered something." I run to my nightstand, open the bottom drawer, and return to the kitchen waving the plate over my head. "It's Mama's china plate."

"Where did that come from?" He runs his finger along the cracks.

"I forgot it was in my drawer. Put it there after I glued it back together." I swallow, then lie, "Mama accidentally broke it." I lay the plate beside the roosters and smile.

"Let's get this mess cleaned up, then I'll go to the hospital."

I take one more glance at the plate, and then pick up a clean dish rag. ❦

~(TWENTY-NINE)~

THE NEXT MORNING Daddy greets me with a Styrofoam cup filled with coffee. "Thought you might like some."

I nod and take a sip. "What time did you get home last night?"

"After nine. I waited at the hospital, hoping to see a doctor, but never did."

I swallow another mouthful, happy at how easy it goes down. "Why are you wearing your dress clothes? Aren't you going to work?"

"Thought I'll go back to the hospital. Maybe they'll let me see your Mama." Before I can ask to go, someone knocks. A vision of the gun-toting boy keeps me a few steps behind Daddy as he opens the door. I peek around to see Mr. Anthony with a large paper sack in each hand, and Sam.

"Good morning, Frank."

"Anthony, morning Samantha. Come on in."

"Actually, I was wondering if you could help me unload Samantha's bicycle."

"Sure."

Sam takes the sacks and walks inside as Daddy follows Mr. Anthony.

"What's wrong?" I ask. "Did your mama do something to you?"

Sam smiles. "No, she hasn't hit me or anything."

"Is she drinking again?"

Sam shakes her head. "She has good days and bad, but she's trying. It's just, well, when I was here yesterday, helping Bea clean up, I realized this is where I belong."

"What'd your mama say about you moving here?"

"Said it's up to me. Think that's part of trying, you know, putting what's best for a person before what's good for yourself."

"Are you gonna stay this time?"

"She'll always be my mama, and I'll visit, may even spend the night every now and then, but this is home."

"Come on then, let's get your stuff put away." I slip my arm through hers, and just like that, have a sister again.

The morning's spent dividing the closet, dresser and desk. Not that Sam has much to put anywhere, but Mr. Anthony promised to take her clothes shopping when he left. Don't know what Mama told that man, but he's been falling all over himself to take care of Sam ever since the morning they talked. Bigger mystery than that, though, is why Miss Clark hasn't kicked him out that fancy house of hers.

"What ya want to do now?"

I shrug. "Doesn't matter."

Sam moves to the window. "Saw some buzzards flying around when we drove up. Let's go catch one."

"How are we supposed to do that?"

"Grab the quilt and follow me."

"I've never heard of a person catching a buzzard with covers off a bed," I say, tossing the pillows on the floor.

Sam's face crunches into a question mark. "That's not to catch 'em with, that's for us to lie down on. Can't believe you've lived in the country all your life and don't know how to do this. What kind of schools did you go to before moving to Pearl?"

"Guess not very good ones. They just taught me how to read, do math, silly stuff like that."

We walk to the middle of the front yard. After checking the sky a few times, she spreads the quilt on the ground and lies down. "Come on and lay on your back like me."

I spread out, keeping my eyes on Sam. "What are we doing?"

"Playing dead. When the buzzards fly down to eat us, we'll grab one."

"You learned this at school?"

"Don't remember exactly where I heard about it. Must have been in science class."

"Have you ever caught a buzzard before?"

"No."

"Do you know anyone that's caught a buzzard this way?"

"Well, no, but I'm sure there's hundreds of folks that have." She looks my direction. "Now, the minute one flies overhead, we've got to get quiet and real still. Move over a little, we need room to stretch our arms out."

"Yeah, all right." I scoot to the edge of the quilt. "Sam, thanks for helping Bea clean up all the glass and stuff."

"Sure," she says, then adds, "were you scared?"

"More afraid of the sheriff than Mama. The way he was waving that gun around, thought for sure it was gonna go off and kill us all."

"That was Tim," Sam says.

"You know him? Is he even old enough to be sheriff?"

"He's a deputy, just stared a couple of weeks ago."

"Well, he needs to go back to sheriff school."

"Yeah, he probably never even went. He's Johnnie Sue's first cousin."

I groan and close my eyes. "Well, that's the end of that then."

"End of what?"

"School, I'm gonna drop out. In fact, I'll never leave the house again. I'm sure the whole town's over at Sunshine right now talking about Mama."

"Maggie, I know you've tried to keep it a secret, but well, you can't change what's happened or what people say, so there's no use frettin' over it. Besides, school doesn't start for a few weeks; by then, they'll be carrying on about something else."

"I just can't stand the 'oh, there's the poor girl with the crazy mama' looks."

"You can't worry about that. Besides, Miss Elizabeth isn't crazy all the time." She squeezes my hand. "She's a good mama, Maggie."

"Yeah, I know. Wish I was as good as you at not caring what people think."

"Look, they're here."

I look up to see three, large, black birds circling overhead. They're too high to see us, but then, they may have unbelievably good eyesight for all I know. "Sam, can they . . ."

"Sh-h-h," she whispers.

We wait, barely breathing for what seems hours. When I'm convinced the buzzards are either blind or too smart to be grabbed, Daddy drives up and they fly away.

"They were getting so close!" Sam moans.

"What birds were you watching?" I ask.

"The ones we were about to catch."

I laugh and stand. "Hey Daddy, how was Mama?" He slams the truck door and shuffles toward the house, head bent.

"Daddy?" He continues the slow walk forward, eyes fixed on the ground. When he reaches the porch step, he stumbles and lands on his knees.

"Mr. Frank!" Sam yells.

We run across the yard, grab an arm and help him stand. "Daddy, what's wrong? Are you sick?" He mumbles a reply, as we walk inside. After he's safely on the couch, I touch his forehead. "Do you have fever? Daddy, do you need to go to the hospital?"

He looks around the room, then closes his eyes. "Elizabeth," he pauses, then whispers, "had a heart attack."

"But, she's not old enough," Sam argues.

I step back. "Daddy, are you sure?"

He looks at me, tears streaming down his face. "She's dead."

Sam screams as darkness closes in on all sides. ~

⤙ THIRTY ⤚

I OPEN MY EYES, heart pounding and listen. There's not one sound. It's been three months and the nightmare still takes my breath away. Staring into the dark, I wait for the images. Daddy kneels before the coffin as Mr. Milton stands guard a few feet away. Mr. Anthony and Miss Clark are on the first row; folks from church, along with my sixth grade teacher, are two rows back; Sam and Colleen are on the back row dabbing their eyes with tissue. Next comes the handshakes and pats as folks whisper how sorry they are for our loss, then, everyone crowds around the hole in the ground. The images, always the same, play through my mind like an old movie.

I ease from bed, careful not to wake Sam, and walk to the window. Not sure what we would have done without Samantha. For weeks after the funeral she reminded us to eat, washed dishes, made beds, even cleaned the floors. She knew when to

talk, when to listen, and when to make Daddy play poker. She
didn't beg when I refused to play cards and somehow always
did exactly what was needed. If only she could bring Mama
back.

"Lord, why did you take her?" I fight to keep my voice low.
"I know you're not going to answer, which by the way, is not
such a great plan. Making us wait till heaven for everything, is
just plain mean." I climb in bed, close my eyes and whisper, "I
need to know she's all right."

I drift to sleep counting all God's many mistakes and don't
wake until late the next morning. A moon pie and note wait on
Sam's pillow, but something keeps me from moving. I squeeze
my eyes shut and search for what's different. It was a new dream.
For once, I wasn't staring at an empty coffin inside Pearl's one
room funeral parlor, or standing in the rain at an empty grave
site. In this dream, I was on a long, wooden pier, and this time,
she was there.

At first, I only saw the clear blue of the lake that extended
out and blended with the sky. I watched sunlight dance across
the sheet of glass and wanted to follow the beams deep beneath
its surface. I walked to the edge of the pier, ready to vanish
into the lake below, when she appeared. Dark hair curled to
her waist, and eyes once deep blue, were now the water that
surrounded us. She took my hand, kissed it softly, and smiled.
It wasn't her everyday smile, but the one splashed across her
face at the beach. The same smile she had for Daddy when they
danced. She tried to walk away, but I wouldn't let her, and for
a moment, the smile disappeared. She cupped my face in her
hand and spoke words I couldn't hear. She said them over and
over until finally I understood. She was happy.

I reach under the bed and remove the box that has remained
closed since the funeral. Until now, I haven't wanted it opened.
I reach for the lid, but stop when the front door slams shut.

"Maggie, you home?"

I leave the box, walk to the kitchen and find Bea with two casserole dishes and a sack from Murray's.

"You just getting out of bed? Land's sakes child, it's almost noon. Don't you have anything better to do than sleep the first day of Christmas break away? Open the refrigerator, will you? I made baked chicken, greens and corn bread for your supper to-night. Don't heat the chicken too long cause you'll dry it out."

"How long are you planning on feeding us?" I ask.

Bea smiles and says, "Until your daddy gets some meat on his bones. Where is he, anyway?"

I shrug. "Probably out back." I sit on the counter and watch my feet dangle.

Bea glances out the window, takes a deep breath, then turns back. "Maggie, that man sure does love you. You're blessed, you know that?"

I want to rattle off the list of why I'm not blessed, including every one of God's failures, but Bea would fall to the floor and pray for six hours straight. I stare at my feet and stay quiet.

She picks up the sack. "Where's Samantha?"

"Left early this morning to visit Colleen."

"You know Samantha's been biting nails about tonight. She wants to attend the Christmas celebration in the worst way, but she's not about to go without you. Y'all should go, Maggie. The whole town comes out, the mayor makes a speech, children sing carols, and the diner even gives out hot chocolate. It'd be good for you to have a little fun. At least think about going."

"Yeah, sure, I'll think about it."

Bea shakes her head, mumbles something I can't make out, and opens the paper bag. "Here, got Miss Clark to pick these up for y'all." She places two white bras on the table. "One's for Samantha. If they don't fit, let me know and she'll exchange 'em."

"Why'd you do that?" I ask, horrified that Miss Clark's now involved with my breasts.

"Don't tell me you haven't noticed your need for one." My face burns and I look back at my feet, as Bea rambles. "Well, I know good and well the boys at your school have noticed. You and Samantha are young ladies now. Try it on when you get a chance, and let me know if it fits."

"All right, thanks," I mumble, still staring at my feet.

"Maggie, you know I'm here if you need to talk about anything."

I grip the edge of the counter. "I'm fine."

"Sure you are, honey. Just want you to know I'm here, is all." She pauses, then says, "Well, I'd better get back. Why don't you come over and help me bake some cookies?"

"Maybe later."

"Wear your coat and gloves when you go out. Might stick a hat on your head too. Weatherman's predicting snow."

I look up. "Are you sure?"

"That's what he said. Could be drinking again, though, because in all my years, I've never seen snow in Pearl." She straightens the red scarf around her neck. "Guess it could mean we're in the last days." She shakes her head and walks out singing *Amazing Grace*.

I move to the window and watch Daddy stare at what's left of Mama's beach. Brown grass has replaced sand, the pool, now empty, leans against the house, and the bridge is on the ground covered with leaves. He stands, looks toward the house, then sits back in the beach chair.

I leave him and return to the box. I remove the perfume bottle and green scarf, placing both on the bed, then remove the poetry book. Taking a deep breath, I flip the pages in search of the last poem she read. When I reach the whippoorwill poem, a typed letter falls onto the floor. I pick it up and read.

Dear Maggie,

I knew you would eventually return to this poem, so I placed the letter here for you to find. I could have told you these things in person, and tried to a number of times, but knew you would be so busy changing my mind that you wouldn't hear my words. This way, they can be read over and over until you understand. Forgiveness may not come until you have a daughter of your own, but hopefully you can appreciate the why behind my words.

There is no greater love on earth, than that of a parent for a child. It calls us to live for someone other than ourselves, and asks us to be deliberate in our choices. It demands more than we have to offer which brings us to our knees in search of wisdom and guidance.

If possible, I would create a world where you would never experience pain, where your deepest desires would become reality and life would meet all of your expectations. Of course, I'm not able to do that, but I can do something more valuable. I can direct you to the God who created you and knows the desires of your heart. A heavenly father who offers strength and peace, and will walk with you through life.

During the first years of illness, I continually asked, Why me? Why this? I begged for healing and grew frustrated when that didn't happen. In about the third year, my questions turned into a prayer. I asked God to use the illness for my good and his glory. I asked for strength to walk in a way that honored him. You see, Maggie, I realized the importance of our responses to the unanswered prayers. I had a choice to either grow bitter and turn away from God, or walk closer allowing his grace to guide each step. I don't know why some things happen the way they do, but I am sure of this: God is loving, and knows what he's doing.

Through my journey, I've been given much. A peace that doesn't depend on circumstances to exist, a joy that remains no matter how difficult life becomes, and an opportunity to be loved deeply. These are the things I want for you. Make it your life's quest to know God. Trust him to answer life's questions in ways that are best for you, accept his love and lean on his strength.

You have shown such determination, never giving up, and have always treated me with tenderness and respect. I'm amazed at how you respond to life with humor, and at your ability to look at those around you honestly. Promise me Mags, never to allow your heart to harden by what you see. Don't let reality crowd out compassion, instead love your way through life, focusing on what's good, and always be honest, because the truth is worth telling.

You may not understand what I'm going to tell you next, but I ask you to honor my request. When I go back to Wakefield, I'll remain there. It's time. I want you and your father to begin new, to have hope of something better. I want you both to be free of the illness. Please give it a try, Mags.

I've made this decision alone, so be mad at me, not at your daddy or God. I'm not sure when I'll see you again, but know that loving you has made me a better person.

Mama

I stare at the letter until words blur, then bury my head and cry for the first time since her death. As tears soak the pillow, I realize they are not for Mama. Her struggle is over. She will never spend another minute in Wakefield or any other crazy hospital. No, the tears are for me and the life I'll never have now that she's gone. I dress slowly, shove the letter into the pocket of my coat and walk outside.

Daddy watches me cross the yard, but doesn't say anything until I sit down and grab his hand. "Mags, are you all right?"

For months, I've barely spoken to him. I wouldn't let him say prayers at night, or turn out the light; I pretended to read while he and Sam played cards, and sat across from him at dinner without even a glance. I took every chance to push him away, because every time I looked at him I saw Mama.

He leans over, wraps his arms around my shoulder and whispers, "I've been waiting for you."

As I push my face into his chest, the wool coat brushes against my skin. "Daddy, I'm so sorry."

"Mags, honey, you don't have a thing to apologize for."

I rest in his arms for a few moments, then lean back against the beach chair. "Did you know Mama wrote me a letter?"

He nods.

"When did she write it?"

"The week-end of your beach party," he says. "She made me promise to put it in the poetry book if she got sick."

"So you knew her plans to live at Wakefield?"

His eyes move to the pool. "I was against it, but your Mama wouldn't listen. She loved us more than she loved herself and was determined we have a life without the illness."

"Is that why she wanted us to move to California?"

"Yeah, she wanted us to begin a new life in your dream city."

"Oh." I blow against my hands.

"I tried to do what she asked, but couldn't. I didn't believe leaving her behind would make our life better. Wouldn't have let her live in Wakefield either."

"What would you have done?"

"I don't know. You know how stubborn your Mama could be. Reckon I would have eventually moved in Wakefield myself."

I watch the worry etched across his face for so long, begin to ease away. "That wouldn't have been a good life. Guess God does know what he's doing."

He smiles and says, "Even when we don't think so."

Cold wind whips through us letting me know the weatherman wasn't drunk after all. "Can you believe it's gonna snow in Pearl?" I ask, rubbing my hands together.

"That's what they're saying."

"Yeah, Bea's never seen it snow and she's been here fifty years. Do you think we're in the end times?"

He laughs. "No, I think it's just cold." He watches me for a moment then says, "You know Maggie, today is December twentieth."

The umbrella leans forward as wind dances across the top. I think of my dream and the way Mama smiled.

"Maggie?"

I brush fresh tears from my face. "It's our Christmas tree day, better get the ax."

Daddy stands. "It's over by the fence. Put it there this morning, just in case. Here put these on."

I slip my hands in the oversized gloves and head toward the woods. We're half-way to the fence when a familiar voice causes us to stop.

"Hey, wait for me." I turn to see Sam looking like Christmas with a green knit hat pulled down right above her eyes, a red coat buttoned to her neck and a plaid scarf trailing behind. She secures the scarf, then runs full speed across the yard stopping a few feet from Daddy. "Where we going?" she asks between gulps of air.

"To cut down our Christmas tree," Daddy says.

"I got home just in time." She twirls around in a circle. "How do you like my new clothes? All this is an early present from Mr. Anthony. There's more over at his house. Got you something too Maggie."

"Really?"

She nods. "So, you like my coat?"

"You're going to be the best dressed person in town tonight."

"Maggie, you mean it?"

I nod. "Will you go, Daddy? The diner's giving away hot chocolate."

"Can't say no to free cocoa."

Sam grabs Daddy's hand. "Mr. Frank, it'll be so much fun. There's even a live Nativity, and since Johnnie Sue's grand-daddy lost the election, she's not playing Mary. This year, a doll will play Jesus. We usually have a real baby, but last year the cow got a little rambunctious and stomped his feet a few times. To hear the town council tell the story, the cow went wild and nearly stepped right on the baby. They called a special meeting the very next day and voted to ban live babies from then on."

Daddy grins. "I'm sure they'll wrap that doll up so good we'll think he's real."

"You're right, Mr. Frank, probably only his little doll eyes will show." She pulls me close to them with her free hand. "Maggie, what kind of tree do you want?"

"I was thinking one that's a little lopsided with a few missing branches."

Sam looks from me to Daddy, and nods. "Well, the decorations will make it look good. Maybe we can string popcorn."

I smile. "It'll be perfect, you'll see."

We cross the fence and I look up at the sky. I don't know why things happen like they do. Not sure why God never took the illness from Mama or why she had to die. I still have a thousand questions, and I'll head to the committee in charge of passing out crosses as soon as I reach heaven. While on earth, though, I'll do my best not to lie. Brother Jim loved to preach about the truth setting a person free. Not sure what that means, but it sounds like something I might need to find out about. Who knows, in time, I might even see the world like Mama. Until then, I'll find one thing each day to be thankful for, no matter how difficult. Today, it's easy. I'm grateful for Daddy, Sam, Bea, and the love they give even when I'm not loveable. That's four things, which means I don't have to think of anything else until Wednesday. Maybe this won't be impossible.

I think of her smile. "She's really fine," I whisper, as snowflakes fall from the sky. ⌇

LaVergne, TN USA
01 October 2010

199258LV00001B/135/P